March woke up sore and ragged, still dressed, but in his own bed this time, not a bathtub, not an alley, not a morgue. Last night had not been a success, exactly, but—All right, not in any sense. But he'd learned some things that might prove helpful. He had a lead or two. Didn't he? He scratched his jaw with his good hand, thought about shaving, thought about going back to sleep, decided he wasn't sleepy anymore. Bone-tired, but not sleepy.

At least things were looking up. In the sense that he wasn't dead. His arm would heal. It was itching more than hurting right now, which had to mean he was out of the woods, right? The part of him that always cautioned him against optimism cautioned him against optimism. But it was hard not to feel he'd been through the worst and come out the other end.

Now it was just a matter of finding Amelia, and he had a promising start on that; then finding out what her connection was to Misty and the world of porn films, and reporting back to the old lady. Then maybe a vacation.

At his front door, he heard a knock. "Just a minute," he called. "Who is it?" And through the door, a friendly voice said, "Messenger service, Holland March home?" A glance through the peephole showed a guy with a genial smile standing there on the stoop.

"Hi," March said, opening the door, and Jackson Healy slugged him full in the face...

The NICE GUYS

a novel by **Charles Ardai**

based on a screenplay
by **Shane Black**
and **Anthony Bagarozzi**

A HARD CASE CRIME NOVEL

A HARD CASE CRIME BOOK

(HCC-S07)

First Hard Case Crime edition: May 2016

Published by

Titan Books
A division of Titan Publishing Group Ltd
144 Southwark Street
London SE1 0UP

in collaboration with Winterfall LLC

This book is a work of fiction. Names, characters, places, and incidents either are the products of the author's imagination or are used fictitiously, and any resemblance to actual events or persons, living or dead, is entirely coincidental.

Print edition ISBN 978-1-78565-257-8
E-book ISBN 978-1-78565-258-5

The name "Hard Case Crime" and the Hard Case Crime logo are trademarks of Winterfall LLC. Hard Case Crime books are selected and edited by Charles Ardai.

Printed and bound by CPI Group (UK) Ltd, Croydon, CR0 4YY

Visit us on the web at www.HardCaseCrime.com

1.

She was old. Most of March's clients were. Foxy chicks walking into a private detective's office with lots of cleavage showing and feathered Farrah hair, that only happened in the movies.

"Do you have a recent picture of your niece you could let me have?" March asked, and the old woman seated across from him, on the overstuffed sofa that smelled like old telephone books—or anyway March imagined it did—blushed pink under her powdered cheeks and her thick glasses. She looked uncomfortable. Embarrassed.

"I'm afraid I do, Mr. March."

March sighed. "You must have something. Any photo at all will be—wait, what?"

The old woman began rummaging in her bag, a yard-wide batik thing with macramé handles that looked as though it could be hiding a family of Chinese immigrants. "I'm very sorry to say I do." From the bag she took a lip-stick container, a compact, a plastic packet containing a folded-up rain bonnet, and set them one by one beside her on the sofa. "Misty was such a *good* child, such a sweet girl, never a bad word out of her mouth. We all expected her to become a nurse, she loved caring for her animals so." The cushion beside her now held a notepad showing Scrabble scores, a tin of lemon pastilles, a spritz bottle of 4711 Eau de Cologne.

"Mrs. Glenn—"

"One moment, young man. I have it here somewhere."

March allowed himself to slump back in the chair. Fuck posture. If a foxy chick ever hired him, he'd sit up straight.

The old lady finished digging in her bag and came up with a folded sheet of glossy paper, like a page torn from a magazine. She unfolded it and held it out to March.

March sat up straight.

The girl in the picture looked to be about twenty-three years old, though it was hard to be sure, with the lighting and the makeup and the feathered Farrah hair. Not to mention the fact that you couldn't look at her face for very long because your eye kept getting drawn lower down to where, holy Christ, were those real? Fuck. It looked like an ad for a porn movie. It *was* an ad for a porn movie. There, in the corner, it said *I Am Sensuous, Lilac. Starring Mi—* The rest was torn off. March forced himself to look away, to look up, to take the photo of the girl in the practically transparent dress with the triple-D bosom and fold it back up and put it in his pocket and say in his most professional voice, "Thank you, Mrs. Glenn. That will be very helpful."

"She told her mother she was acting in movies," the old lady said. "We thought she meant the sort we watched with her growing up. *The Wizard of Oz. The Sound of Music.*"

"Well," March said, "some of these sorts of movies have music in them."

Lily Glenn fixed him with a stony stare.

"You didn't mention that your niece was an…adult performer," March said. "What name did she work under?"

"Oh, Misty," Mrs. Glenn said. Her voice fell. "Misty Mountains."

At which point something clicked in March's brain and he sat up straighter still. He didn't watch all that much television, but every so often he caught a glimpse, mostly in bars, and one glimpse he'd caught a few days earlier had been a local news report about a porn actress who'd died in a rather spectacular car crash somewhere near Coldwater Canyon. He hadn't focused on the name, these porn chicks all had similar sounding names, but now that he heard it again, well. Mountains. Misty Mountains. No doubt a reference to her love of the great outdoors.

"I'm so sorry, Mrs. Glenn," March said, and it sounded mechanical, and he felt a little bad about that, but he barreled on. "I'm sorry for your loss. But didn't you say you saw your niece just the other day?"

"Yes."

"You mean before the, um, before the accident?"

"No. After."

"But…Mrs. Glenn…didn't your niece, you know, *die* in that accident?"

The old lady meticulously gathered up the things from the sofa, dropped them one by one back into her bag. "Obviously not," she said.

"Obviously not," March said. "Obviously not."

"I saw her, Mr. March. Plain as day, through the window of her house, sitting at her desk, in a blue pinstripe jacket, writing something. But when I knocked…"

"When you knocked?"

The old lady shrugged, and all the air seemed to go out of her. She was a deflated balloon, tethered by one hand to the batik monstrosity beside her. "She ran away. Out the back door. Jumped in a car and raced off. I called to her, you understand, I shouted, but she didn't hear."

Or heard and didn't want to stop, March thought.

"Can you describe the car?"

"It was red," Mrs. Glenn said.

"And…?"

She shrugged again and looked helplessly at March.

"Four doors? Two? Little Japanese job? Big old Detroit gas guzzler?"

Another shrug.

"Don't you remember anything about the car at all, Mrs. Glenn?"

"Well, there was one thing," the old lady said. "I don't know if it's helpful, but I wrote it down." She went rummaging in her bag again. "I think you call it the license plate number?"

2.

This is how it went down:

It was somewhere between ten PM and midnight, Mulroney didn't know when exactly, he could look it up, but fuck it, right? What does it matter? Night's night. Point is, it was dark out, and the kid's parents were asleep, and do you want to hear the story or not?

March wanted to hear the story.

So it's dark out, the father's an orthopedist, spent the day fixing bunions, the mother's a whatchacallit, a, a, Jesus fucking Christ, he couldn't think of the word, anyway it kept her on her feet all day, so she's bushed too, and the kid—Bobby's his name, Bobby Vandruggen, the pop's Henry, the mom's Joyce—sometimes your memory works, sometimes it doesn't, right?—anyway, the kid's up because, you know, it's only ten PM—

Or midnight.

Or fucking eleven twenty-eight, point is he's awake, and he's watched the Hardy Boys, he's watched that Steve Austin show, sure he could watch Carol Burnett, but he's a teenage boy and his parents are asleep so you know what he's gonna do instead, am I right? So he sneaks into his parents' room, because he knows where the old man stashes the good stuff, right under the bed, copies of *Rogue* and *Oui* and *Snizz* where the lady of the house'll never find 'em, 'cause when does she ever clean under the bed, right? So mom and pop are sawing logs, and little Bobby sneaks in quiet as a goddamn mouse and snatches whatever's on top, only I can tell you what it was because we entered it into evidence, didn't we? Can't leave shit like that lying around, can we?

Of course not.

Of course not. So it's like a year-old issue of *Cavalier*—don't give me that look, like you never bought a copy, March.

Never in my life.

Should try it sometime. Anyway, little Bobby takes his prize to the kitchen and makes himself a sandwich and he carries it to the living room and he sits on the couch in his button-fly pajamas, and opens to the centerfold, which this month is Misty Mountains, and if you say you don't know who that is, I swear to god, March, I'm gonna start thinking you're a fruit. Don't answer that, I don't even want to know.

Now, meanwhile—this is up by Mulholland, right? On the hillside? And up on the highway, this blue Trans Am comes out of nowhere, takes the curve at maybe eighty, I'm talking real *Smokey and the Bandit*-type shit here. Smashes through the guardrail, *bang*, starts tearing down the hill, right toward the kid's house, where the orthopedist and his lady are sleeping and their boy is focused on Misty Mountains. Can you imagine? Then, *boom*, the whole fucking side wall of his house comes down, and this Trans Am comes tearing through. Miracle he wasn't under the wheels, you want to know the truth. Place is a total goddamn disaster area. Car goes right through an armchair, a grandfather clock, the wall on the other side—*bam*, *bam*, *bam*. Half the ceiling comes down. Mom and pop wake up, of course. They're calling his name, Bobby, Bobby, but Bobby's outside, running down the hill, to where the car's fetched up against this stand of trees. And the driver, get this, she's been thrown, she's lying on the ground next to the open door, the car's totaled and she's pretty badly fucked up too, barely breathing, but she's—you won't fucking believe this— completely, bare-ass, like a bluebird, naked. I mean, *nothing* on. You understand? I'm not saying she went driving in her panties. I mean *nothing*. And who do you fucking think it is?

Misty Mountains.

What, you already heard this?

It was on the news, Mulroney. Everyone's heard it.

Well, I'll tell you something you didn't hear on the news. She's dying, right? She's got barely enough breath to speak, but she's trying to get something out, and the boy leans close to hear it. You want to know what she says to him? This naked lady he'd just been whacking off to, who just wrecked his house, who's lying by the steaming, crumpled wreck of her Trans Am? She takes one last breath and says to him, she says, "How do you like my car, big boy?"

I shit you not, March.

And then she dies. Right in front of him. And you know what this kid does? He pulls off his pajama top, and he covers her up with it. Not like over her face, over those beautiful tits of hers. So she's decent, you know? When mom and pop get there. When Stevenson and Pickler show up.

That's how it went down, according to Officer William Mulroney of the LAPD, while he looked up the license plate number of a red '74 Volkswagen Type 181 registered to one Amelia Francine Kuttner.

3.

Somewhere on the way to forty, Jackson Healy felt he'd taken a wrong turn, but the thing was, if he tried to pin down just when and where, he couldn't. It's not like there'd been anything so bad about his life—I mean, there'd been plenty of bad things, but *so* bad? Lots of people had it worse, some of them because of Jackson Healy. So if he was being totally honest about it, he didn't have much to complain about. He had enough work, he got by. He had his room above the Comedy Store, where Mitzi comped him his ginger ales. He had his fish to take care of, which heaven knows was better than having a cat or a dog. Or a person. And when people came to him and asked him for help, he helped.

Not that he was an altruist or anything. (*Altruism*, noun: the impulse to help other people, unselfishly. Not every word his Word-a-Day calendar taught him was useful, but that one had been. It had made him stop and think.) He wasn't unselfish. It was a job. He had a rate, and people paid it or he didn't take the work. Early on, he'd let people pay on the come, after he'd done his part, but more than once they'd reneged, or tried to, and that just meant he'd had to explain to them why that wasn't the way you did business. And the lesson took, of course— he'd gotten paid in the end—but it was like having to do two jobs for one fee, and where's the sense in that? So

now it was pay up front, cash on the barrelhead, or Healy
would just take himself upstairs and feed the fish, and
you could find some other way to take care of the guy
who was threatening you, or messing around with your
underage daughter, or whatever it was.

That said, Healy did like to help. That day in the
diner—no one had been paying him then. Now, it's not
like he'd had much choice: that fucker with the shotgun
had been out of his goddamn mind, flying so high on PCP
or acid or some goddamn thing that he thought the new
Grand Slam breakfast they'd introduced was a plot against
white people in general and him in particular. But you
know, there were at least a dozen people in that Denny's
at the time and nothing said Healy had to be the one to
vault the counter and tackle the son of a bitch. Someone
else could've taken the shot in the fucking bicep. The
thing is, no one else did. Everyone else was screaming
and turning over tables and hiding behind them. And
Healy could've done that too, his bicep would've thanked
him if he had. But what he did instead was stand up and
take a flying leap at a crazy motherfucker with a shotgun
in his hands and not one but two fingers on the trigger.

He'd been on the news after that, people from as far
away as Oregon had called to say they saw him, flat on his
back on an ambulance gurney, his shirt perforated and
soaked with blood, grinning as they wheeled him off. And
why'd he been grinning? Because it felt good. Not his
arm, lord knows, not the prospect of six weeks of recovery
with no painkillers. But what he'd done. Like it was a step
up or something. It was still beating on people, still using

his fists to solve problems, but for a purpose, not a paycheck.

His sponsor, Scotty, told him maybe it meant he was ready to move on, try a different line of work, which maybe it was. Healy had thought for a couple years now about maybe applying for his investigator's license, working under an experienced P.I. for a while, then opening his own office, his own business, ad in the Yellow Pages and everything. Those guys help people. It'd feel good to wake up in the morning knowing that's what was on the docket for the day.

But with one thing and another, he hadn't done it, and he was starting to wonder if he ever would. Maybe the life he had was the right life for him, like a suit of clothes you wouldn't see on any magazine covers but that fit you without pinching here or squeezing there. It may not be what you set out to wear, but it's what you had in your closet.

Ambition's a funny thing. When he'd been a kid, practicing on his brother's guitar up in the attic, he'd thought he'd be Bill Haley when he grew up. Where had that gone? It hadn't been lack of talent, it had been lack of desire. Well, maybe lack of talent too. But he'd never even had the chance to fail for that reason, since lack of desire had taken him out of the race first.

Eh. Healy tossed back the last of his ginger ale, got up from the stool he'd been occupying while watching the clock behind the bar, dropped some change beside his glass, and grabbed a handful of peanuts for the road. Who wanted to be Bill Haley anyway. Look how the man

wound up, just another drunk with a spit curl and some
memories.

Three PM, school would be out soon, time to go to work.

The girl's name was Kitten, and maybe that was where
the problem started. Who names their little girl Kitten?
But this was California and the sixties weren't so far in
the rear-view mirror and every middle school had its
share of Kittens and Rainbows and such. This one's father
seemed nothing but sensible and concerned when you
sat down across a table from him now, but who knows
what he'd been smoking back in '64 when Kitten was
conceived?

Hell, from what he could smell right now, Healy decided little Kitten wasn't above a toke or two herself.

Healy was installed beneath a window, hugging the
flagstone side wall of a Ventura County two-story, where
he was hidden by the late-afternoon shadow. They were
upstairs, Kitten and her swain, in a back bedroom, and the
window was open halfway, with just a fluttering curtain to
keep bugs out. This meant Healy was not only getting a
noseful, he could hear them too, and it was a conversation for the ages.

"Who's the man, baby?" came the drawling male voice.
"Who ?"

And Kitten answered, "You are, you're the man, oh yes,
you're the man. You! You!"

Healy ate a peanut.

He'd picked up Kitten's trail as she came down the
steps of her school building on Sepulveda, laughing with

two other girls about some filmstrip they'd just watched in English class, apparently a super-lame one. They were probably all the same age, but looking at them Healy understood why it was Kitten's dad who had felt the need to hire him. There's thirteen and then there's thirteen. Kitten had a long, lush sweep of chestnut hair, down past her shoulders, cherry-red lips, a face that would turn heads anywhere she went and a look on it that said she knew damn well it would. Precocious, Healy supposed you'd call it, except all kids these days were precocious, and this was something beyond that. Kids like Kitten knew too much and too little all at the same time.

She picked up her bicycle from a rack of others just like it—tassels on the handlebars, banana seat—and pedaled hard to reach a drive-in restaurant half a mile away. Then she sat and waited for someone to drive in, and it turned out to be a man three times her age in a two-tone convertible.

Sue Lyon had nothing on our Kitten, except that pair of heart-shaped sunglasses. Which Kitten really didn't need. Her little tan shorts and lazily gapping crop top did the job just as well, and if they hadn't, the expression in her eyes and her winsome pout would have. Healy watched from across the street, and when Kitten climbed into the convertible, Healy got in his own car and followed.

Which is how he'd wound up here, peeping at the window, or more precisely sitting around under the window, waiting for it all to be over.

"You're the man," Kitten squealed, "you're my foxy-fox!"

Healy winced.

"Foxy-fox! Foxy-fox!"

Okay, he's your foxy-fox. But tell me, is he the man…?

"Oh, yes baby! Yes! You're the man, baby!"

Well, there you go.

Healy shelled another peanut. It was impossible not to think back to his own brief flirtation with marriage. If that had lasted, if he and June had had a kid, she might have been about this girl's age now. And would their kid have turned out any better? Probably not, given her mother's influence. The last conversation Healy had ever had with June, she'd kicked things off with this doozy of an ice-breaker: "Jack? I'm fucking your dad."

More peanuts. Kitten reappeared a few minutes later outside the house, wheeling her bicycle down to the road. Healy watched her climb on and pedal off. From inside the house came the sound of a shower turning on. He really didn't want to wait for the guy to finish his ablutions (noun, the washing of one's body, esp. ritually), so Healy strolled over to the front door, reached into his jacket pocket, pulled out the pair of brass knuckles he had stashed there, and slipped them on over his fingers. They were a comforting weight in his hand. He used them to knock on the door.

A pause, then footsteps approached the other side of the door. Healy heard the peephole cover slide back, put a genial smile on his face, lowered the hand he'd knocked with so it was out of sight.

The door swung open partway. The man stood there in

a red silk bathrobe, loosely belted and open to his navel.
Up close he looked even older.

"So you're the man, huh?" Healy said.

The man's face scrunched up. "What?"

Healy drew his arm back, let go with a right cross that
shattered the man's jaw.

4.

On the way home, knucks wiped and put away again, Healy stopped at a stretch of pavement off Mulholland Drive. He was late, nearly twenty minutes late, but the new client he'd arranged to meet hadn't given up on him. She was sitting in the driver's seat of her red VW convertible, waiting as Healy walked over.

She had hair about as long and dark and attractive as Kitten's, and was roughly as beautiful, but where Kitten clearly had not a care in her thirteen-year-old head, this woman had a decade's more acquaintance with life and seemed deeply anxious. Which of course made sense when you heard her story.

"I think there's two of them," she said, and she handed a slip of paper out the window to him. It was pink and shaped like a cow, with a few lines scrawled on it in ballpoint. "I just got the name and description for one. They've been talking to all my friends, asking where I live. Mr. Healy—I'm scared."

While Healy studied the slip, the girl got an envelope from the handbag on the seat beside her. She handed it to him.

"You'll take care of them?" she asked.

Healy took the envelope. "Consider it done."

"Thank you," she said, and he could hear the relief in

her voice. "Honestly, I feel better already. You…you make me feel safe."

Healy smiled, thought about the whole private investigator thing. Maybe. Someday. "That's my job," he said, trying it on for size, and turned away, thumbing open the envelope as he went. He paused, counting the money. Turned back. "Um…you're short."

"Excuse me…? I'm what?"

He held up the envelope. "You're seven bucks short."

"Oh," the girl said.

"Yeah."

She started fishing in her purse. "I'm sorry…here, hang on…"

Because he wasn't a fucking altruist, that's why.

5.

Morning found Holland March asleep, still fully dressed from the night before, in his blue serge suit, silk tie, patterned shirt. He was submerged to the neck in lukewarm water in his bathtub. It had been properly warm when he'd gotten in, a few hours after midnight, but had cooled since. He had been out drinking and had come home alone.

He woke to the sound of his daughter's voice coming through the loudspeaker of his telephone answering machine, a new device he'd hooked up just the week before, which eliminated the need for the answering service he'd used until then. That was fifteen dollars a month he could stop spending. Holly was saying something over the recording of his voice, which was reciting, "You have reached March Investigations. This machine records messages. Wait for the tone, and speak clearly." There was a beep. Then a pause. Then Holly started in again.

"This is your daughter speaking," she said. "Thursday, as you may remember, is my birthday. Please give accordingly—"

March put one hand on each side of the tub and heaved himself up. He glanced at his fingers—pruney. Very, very pruney. And what was that on his palm? He looked more closely. Written across his right hand in permanent marker, the handwriting unfamiliar but feminine:

You will never be happy

"—also, I hope you didn't forget you're supposed to be working today. Because, you know. Bills."

March heard the phone go click. Then another beep and the whirr of the cassette tape advancing.

His temples throbbed.

Work.

Yeah.

He started unbuttoning his sopping shirt.

Gas lines were good for one thing: they gave you time to catch up on the news. On the radio of his beat-up Mercedes convertible, some lady reporter was at the L.A. Auto Show, interviewing an industry rep named Bergen Paulsen who clearly just wanted to bullshit with her about the new makes and models they'd be showing off at the big opening night event, but she wanted to be Woodward and Bernstein rolled into one, peppering him with questions about emissions and smog control and yadda yadda yadda. Meanwhile, the newspaper March had grabbed on his way out the door was reporting on the progress of those killer bees that were supposedly coming up from South America to end life as we knew it. Those fucking bees had supposedly been coming for years now, newspapers had been scaring people about them since Nixon was in office, and had they ever shown up, even one of them? At least the smog you could see out there.

March looked at the smog.

Yep, it was hanging over the city like a white quilt that had spent too many years on a smoker's bed. You looked at the air and pictured it going into your lungs and it was enough to make you sick. At least he couldn't smell it anymore, not since that dickhole he'd been tailing last summer clocked him in the back of the head with a board studded with rusty nails. Was it the rust that did it, or just the concussion? The docs didn't know. Would his sense of smell return someday? Maybe. In the meantime, smog didn't stink, and neither did the gasoline everyone was lined up to buy, but you know what? He couldn't smell roses either, and his wife was dead. So.

March reached under the front seat, retrieved a battery-operated electric razor, Holly's gift to him last Christmas, and clicked it on. Went to work on his stubble, let the noise of the motor drown out the honking of the cars around him as they inched angrily toward the pumps. Somewhere up front, near the head of the line, two drivers had gotten out of their cars and were shouting at each other. Fists were getting waved in faces. You might think, with an energy crisis going on, people would save their energy. Maybe even band together or something. Help their fellow man. But, no. People were still mean, and petty, and unforgiving. And a good thing, too, as far as March was concerned, because if that ever changed he'd be out of a job.

As it was, nearly half his business had gone away, the result of California implementing no-fault divorce. No longer did you need pictures of your hubby screwing his secretary, or your wife schtupping the milkman, or you know, vice versa, before a judge would let you call it quits. And just like that, half the private cops in California were out of work. Probably leading to more than a few divorces, which were simpler now, so, there you go, silver lining. But the point was, if you wanted to make a living as a private eye these days, you had to hustle for it. Which was why March had become such a frequent visitor at the place where he'd met Lily Glenn, the Leisure World retirement park, where his buddy Rudy ran security. Rudy was happy to fund his losing bets on every nag that ran at Santa Anita with the ten percent March kicked back to him any time one of the residents hired him to find a missing spouse or whatnot. It was easy work. Most of the time the missing spouse could be found resting in an urn on the mantelpiece, his demise having conveniently been forgotten by his loving wife of fifty-seven years.

And maybe Mrs. Glenn's sighting of her beloved niece, writing at a desk in her house several days after she died in a car crash, fell into this category. People saw what they wanted to see, especially when they were on four or five prescriptions and peered at the world through bifocals. It would be easy enough for March to generate a report saying he'd looked into it, conducted a thorough investigation, and, no, Misty really was gone, so sorry. Mrs. Glenn would have a good cry and get over it, and her fee would pay for Rudy's latest flight of fancy at the track, the laundry bills for March's blue suit, and maybe even a birthday present for Holly. A good day's work all around.

But.

But—sometimes people weren't just seeing things,

even old people, even nearsighted old people. And the
fact was, that license plate number she'd dutifully written
down? It was a real number, registered to a real car, and
what were the odds she could pull something like that
out of her wrinkly ass?

Which left March with a goddamn quandary. Namely
was he going to track down this Amelia Francine Kuttner
and her mystery car and ask what she'd been doing in the
deceased's house? Or was he going to say fuck it and go
back to sleep, in a proper bed this time, either his own or,
preferably, one belonging to a woman of the female persuasion?

Later in the day it would've been a toss-up. But it was
early still and bars wouldn't be open for a while yet, and
women wouldn't show up in them for a while longer, and
he'd taken Lily Glenn's money, not that that meant much,
but it meant something, maybe. And damn it, he was
curious now. What *was* this Amelia doing in a dead porn
star's house?

He pulled up at last to the Arco station at the end of
the line, and made a decision he'd live to regret.

The tag number had led to an address (thank you, Officer
Mulroney), a dive in West Hollywood, up a flight of stairs
from a doughnut shop that insisted on spelling its wares
"DONUT," which March fucking hated. The spelling,
not the doughnuts. The doughnuts were fine, he ate a
couple and called it breakfast, then climbed to the landing.

He looked left and right before kneeling in front of
Amelia's door and eyeballing the lock to see if it was the

simple sort he could pick. It turned out to be the even simpler sort he could open just by turning the knob. Inside, anything that could ever have been stolen clearly already had been. The place was picked clean. A mattress on the floor had no sheet on it, no blanket, no pillow. Even so, March was briefly tempted. But he moved on.

The bathroom had one lonely toothbrush lying on the rim of the sink. The kitchen was empty except for a rusty fridge humming in one corner. He checked the freezer compartment, because you never knew, people had been known to keep valuables in their ice cube trays, but this chick didn't. She did have an untouched pint of Baskin-Robbins rum raisin, which March would've taken a crack at but, no spoon.

That was it, three rooms, no furniture to speak of. The closet was bare. Nothing taped to the walls. He was on his way out the door when something occurred to him and he went back to the mattress and lifted it by one corner.

At first he thought the little rectangle adhering to the underside was a label, but it slipped off, came fluttering down, landed on the floor like a fall leaf. A business card.

March picked it up.

THE EROTIC CONNECTION, it said in cheerful bubble letters, shiny with foil stamping. And written in ballpoint ink on the back, *Tue 6pm.*

6.

Now as it happened, March knew a thing or two about the Erotic Connection.

Back when he'd been on the force, fresh faced and in his twenties, he'd done a tour on the stretch of Santa Monica that was home to the Pink Pussycat. Alice Schiller ran the place, and lest you think less of Holland March for stopping in for a beverage and some cheering conversation at the end of a long shift, you've got to remember, everyone in Hollywood used to go there at one time or another. Fucking *Sinatra* went there. This wasn't some two-bit clip joint. It was at least a four- or five-bit clip joint, and Alice ran it as den mother and seductress and CEO and yenta combined. She kept the booze flowing and the girls on their game. Even brought Lenny Bruce's mom in to teach classes—painted right on the wall of the building it said in huge letters

THE PINK PUSSYCAT
COLLEGE OF STRIPTEASE
OL 4 - 0280

and if a girl dialed that number, she was in for a better education than she'd get at Scripps or Mount St. Mary's.

Now, when a girl had gone through the program, she was expected to put her newfound skills and knowledge to work on Alice's behalf—unless, of course, she met a husband at the club, that was another story, then Alice would pop a bottle of champagne and all the girls would celebrate her good fortune. But you weren't supposed to just pick up and carry yourself to another nightclub a few blocks away, and you certainly weren't supposed to take three of the other girls with you when you did.

Which is what Betty Bramden had done, when a boyfriend of hers decided to open the Blue Bird Club, a less classy version of the same concept. Less 1940s, more 1960s; less burlesque, more Summer of Love. But it was the Pink Pussycat all over again in all the ways that counted, and Alice was having none of it. She hadn't been pouring for her various police friends on the arm all this time for nothing, and she let it be known that she was very concerned about the new element the Blue Bird was bringing into the neighborhood, bad characters, the kind that'd get into fights in the parking lot after last call, and were those needles she'd seen thrown in the gutter out front?

They were needles all right, and March knew that because he was the one who'd thrown them there. Just a handful, but enough to fill a glassine envelope with the LAPD stamp on it and get Betty Bramden's boyfriend led out in cuffs.

With one thing and another, the Blue Bird was closed inside of a month, and though he was never one hundred percent certain that Alice knew what he had done for her or would have approved if she had known, he hadn't said no when, in an abundance of high spirits on the day the Blue Bird shut down for good, she'd introduced him to a girl called Ruth Dubitsky, who danced under the name

Heady Lamarr and proved true to the name when the dressing room door closed behind them.

Which has what to do with the Erotic Connection, you wonder.

Well.

Couple of years in prison and the boyfriend turned himself into quite the jailhouse lawyer, and he never stopped claiming, in letter after letter to the DA's office, to the newspapers, to anyone who would listen, that he'd been set up. Eventually he found a way to get his conviction vacated, and while no one ever told March his badge was on the line for it, the fact was, March had been a cop at one point and now he wasn't, and the boyfriend had been a jailbird and now he wasn't. You might think, after that experience, the man would go into another line of work, but leopards, spots. He opened a new club just a few miles away from where the Blue Bird had been, updated the décor to be less Summer of Love and more *Joy of Sex*, and he called it the Erotic Connection.

7.

Which was why March wanted nothing to do with the place.

But—you don't find a business card in the emptied-out apartment of a woman you're looking for, a business card with something written on it, and just throw it in the trash and call it a day. Not if you're a private detective. There are plenty of ways to make a living, plenty of better ways than being a private detective, and he hadn't chosen any of them. March wasn't the philosophical sort and wouldn't talk your ear off about how some professions you don't choose, they choose you, at least not unless he had a whole bunch of drinks in him; but the simple truth of the matter was, the kind of person who gets his P.I. license could no more ignore that business card, having found it, than he could have tap danced across the Grand Canyon.

So, leery though he was, wary though he was, March headed downtown to the Erotic Connection. It was 1PM by the time he arrived, and the doors were open, though no actual customers were inside. March had watched from across the street for a bit, through the window of a drugstore, but you couldn't see in, of course, so all he could say for sure was that no one he recognized had entered or left in the past fifteen minutes.

He crossed briskly, pulled open the door, and went in.

His eyes took a minute to adjust. The bar was a modern one, all chrome trim and glass, with big wooden speakers mounted up by the ceiling above it and a disco ball lazily turning just beyond. The frosted squares of the dance floor were lit from underneath, blinking on and off, on and off. There was no music playing, and the only girls in sight were the ones painted on the walls.

"What are you having?" This from the bartender, who stood wiping down the counter with a rag.

March ordered a beer, got right into it as soon as he'd taken his first swallow. "You know a girl named Amelia? Amelia Kuttner?"

Got a blank look for his trouble.

"She's a brunette, about yea high…?" He held his hand up at about the level of the bartender's chin. "Hair down to here…?" So far, he could've been describing Misty Mountains, but then that was the point, wasn't it? The aunt hadn't mistaken this girl for her niece for no reason. Of course, the aunt hadn't seen her from the front. Odds were Amelia didn't have *all* the same physical features Misty had, because how many women did. But the aunt had definitely said dark hair, yea high. "Lives in the neighborhood, or used to, anyway?" Nothing. "Might have met someone here last Tuesday, or the Tuesday before? Some Tuesday…?"

The bartender shook his head. So far, the only five syllables the man had spoken were the ones asking March for his drink order. For all he knew, the man didn't speak English and had learned them phonetically. Maybe he just drew the same beer for you no matter what you ordered.

"Can I show you a photograph…?"

"Friend," a voice said, and a heavy hand landed on March's shoulder. "Drink your drink and let the man do his job, will you?"

March turned on the bar stool, followed the line of the man's arm to his shoulder, to the wide lapels of his pristine white jacket, to the burgundy collar of his silk shirt, and from there up to the man's chin and lips and nose and eyes. He felt like he was assembling a profile out of pieces, like an identikit. He got to the little blue jailhouse tattoo of a cross beneath the man's right eye before recognition clicked in, and he could see it click for the man, too, at the same instant.

"You—"

Which of them had said it? Both of them had. And the man's grip tightened on March's shoulder.

March tensed, started to say something, but found himself drawn forward, his chest pressed against the other man's, his ear close to the other man's lips. "After all this time," Marcus Breydo said. "All these years. You walk into my club."

"Um," March said, and wished he was carrying. "About that—"

"Shh," Breydo said. "It's all right. I've found him, too."

"Him?"

"Christ Jesus," the former boyfriend of Betty Bramden, inveterate strip club impresario, said, releasing his grip on March's torso, stepping back, and aiming two fingers at his tattoo. "I've been reborn in his blood, brother. I've begged forgiveness of every man I've wronged, as I forgive those who trespassed against me. We're all sinners." He squinted at March. "It's why you sought me out, isn't it?"

"Hallelujah," March said.

After which he got stood a drink and had to hear about Breydo's conversion, which seemed to have involved a combination of Bible verses and power-lifting on the yard. Not to mention the safety pin dipped in ballpoint ink giving him the permanent mark of the brotherhood. March nodded a lot, and tried not to look like the kid in Sunday school who wished he was out playing with his friends instead.

"So, man, go ahead," Breydo finally said, "ask me what you came to ask me."

March opened his mouth. Closed it. Opened it again.

"Go ahead," Breydo said.

"Do you," March said, "do you, um, forgive me?"

"Yes, brother. Yes. I do. I do forgive you."

And there was hugging again, which went on long enough that March really needed it to stop. But, gift horses. He let the other man take the lead.

"Can I ask you one other thing?" March said when the strip club owner finally let go.

"Yes, brother. Yes. Ask me anything."

March took the folded photo out of his pocket. "Do you know a girl named Amelia…?"

8.

He did.

Knew her from the description, remembered hearing her name. She had been there a week ago Tuesday, meeting a man who worked in movies, guy named Rocco, in the distribution end of the business. Dirty movies, the real hardcore stuff. Not a Christian like you and me, brother. Not yet, anyway. Right? God's grace comes to all in time.

March nodded. He was getting so good at it.

They'd been talking about something, some project— not that he'd been *listening*, they just hadn't been talking very quietly, understand?

"A movie project? A porn film…?"

Breydo shook his head. "I don't know, it was confusing. Yeah, there was a movie, something about a movie, but also some political thing, maybe some radio thing? She kept talking about doing something on the air."

"On the air?"

"That's what she said. Her and these other people. She asked if he wanted to meet her crew, said they'd be meeting later on."

Did Breydo know where…?

That had led him here, to the Iron Horse, in the same zip code as the Erotic Connection but a place of an entirely different stripe. No naked women on the walls here. This was a drinking establishment, and the people in it (and yes, it was relatively full already in the early afternoon) were established drinkers. It was blue collar and no-nonsense, though there was a university campus nearby, and as a concession to the student population there was a crowded bulletin board you passed on the way in, full of mimeographed sheets promoting local gigs and bands and protests and whatnot, all stabbed into the cork with pushpins. March flipped through a few layers. On the air, on the air… He pulled one flyer down, folded it, jammed it in his pocket, went on in.

The bartender at the Iron Horse looked like he'd been a bruiser once, but that was before he got a job that gave him access to free liquor. He wore a salmon-colored shirt and wore it open, to give his belly a chance to breathe.

"I think I remember her," he said, leaning forward on his meaty fists. "Amelia. She was in three, four nights ago. With a tall guy? They sat here for a while, waiting for her friends to show. Drank bourbon martinis." He said this last with a trace of distaste.

"Disgusting," March said, though he wouldn't have turned one down. "Was the guy buying?"

"He bought some, she bought some."

"Don't suppose they paid with credit cards, did they?"

The meaty fists rose from the bar, turned into crossed arms across the man's chest. "As in, am I going to pull the receipts for you? Fat fucking chance."

March dug in his pocket, held out a folded ten-dollar bill. Folded to look like a little origami shirt. Sometimes it helped to make 'em laugh a little.

"That's very pretty," the bartender said.

"I made it myself."

"Yeah?" the bartender said. "I made this." And he reached under the bar, came up with a carved wooden bat. Like a Louisville Slugger, only heavier.

March nodded, tucked the bill back in his pocket.

But there was more than one way to skin a cat, like March's mother always said. Which had been pretty annoying, actually. She used that expression entirely too much. But here it applied. Anyway. If there were credit card receipts that might reveal another address for Amelia, or one for this Rocco, he needed to get his hands on them.

So: he was crouching in the alleyway behind the Iron Horse, next to a dumpster he assumed was probably reeking, but fuck it, he couldn't smell a thing, waiting for the lights to go out and the steel gate over the front door to come clattering down. He heard it at last, then footsteps receding, and it was just March and the back door, alone together in the night.

The knob didn't turn this time, that would've been too much to hope for, but there was a glass panel in the door, not even any chicken-wire reinforcement in the glass, and March figured it wouldn't be too difficult to smash the thing in. That's what they did on TV, wasn't it? March looked in the dumpster, pulled out a scrap of cloth that didn't look too dirty, started wrapping it around his knuckles. Noticed the writing on his hand again, *You will never be happy*, fainter than this morning but still there. We'll see about that, honey. Gonna earn myself another bonus payment. And he smashed his wrapped fist through the glass.

No alarms sounded, just the tinkle of shards against the ground. This was the part where he was supposed to reach through the opening, turn the handle from inside, let himself in, find the box of receipts behind the bar, rifle through them by the glare of his penlight, pick out the two he wanted, maybe mutter *Bingo* under his breath, let himself out, wipe down the knob, and beat leather back to March Investigations HQ, aka home. But his wrist hurt.

He looked down. He was bleeding.

"Ow, shit. Shit." He pressed two fingers of his other hand against his wrist.

Blood seeped through around them.

"Ow, ow, ow." He pulled the rag from around his knuckles, wound it around his wrist instead. It soaked through instantly. "Whoa. Ow. Whoa. Lots of blood. Lots of blood. Okay. Okay."

He glanced around the alley, staggered a few steps. He was feeling dizzy.

Goddamn, that was a lot of blood.

He shifted his grip on his wrist, and a literal jet of blood came spraying up.

"Okay. Ow. Wait, wait. Okay. Okay."

He was teetering in a tight little circle. Or maybe it just felt that way. His eyes started to flutter. Blood all over the place.

The end of the alley wasn't so very far, was it? How could it be that far?

Feet.

Come on.

Jesus.

9.

He came to in an ambulance, an oxygen mask strapped to his face, the siren screaming.

He felt the gurney under him bang against the sides as they slalomed through traffic.

His wrist still hurt.

There was a medic hunched over him, a tiny Latina fireplug, shouting, but the words were strangely quiet, like his ears were stuffed with cotton batting.

"I need two units of whole blood! Shit! BP dropping! Stay with me, stay with me—"

March didn't listen to any more. Why should he. It was Thanksgiving, and the turkey smelled so good, fresh from the oven, and the candied yams. How a Brit like his wife ever learned to cook Thanksgiving dinner like that he had no idea, but there you go, she was a talented lady. And Holly had blown out the candles on her cake, and what are you talking about, you smell gas?

And he was out, like a pilot light.

10.

The night was quiet now, which was probably because it was morning.

Barely any cars went by on the highway outside the hospital, and the few that did swooshed past almost in silence, the sound of their tires against the pavement like ocean surf.

March sat in his wheelchair and waited quietly while the hospital nun locked the wheels.

It took a while for the cab he'd called to show up.

When it did, the nun helped him stand.

His wrist was thickly bandaged.

"Tell me," the nun said as she led him to the taxi, "are you willing to find God?"

It was funny, most days no one talked to him about God. Now in one day he got Breydo and this chick.

He struggled to speak, his brain still fogged by all the painkillers they'd pumped into him.

"I'm…I'm still trying to find Amelia."

He sank into the cab's back seat, gave his address to the driver. They drove off.

When he got home, Holly was there, awake, ready to lead him in and tuck him into bed. She was a good kid. He didn't deserve her.

*

He woke up eleven hours later, sore and ragged, still dressed, but in his own bed this time, not a bathtub, not an alley, not a morgue. Last night had not been a success, exactly, but— All right, not in any sense. But he'd learned some things that might prove helpful. He had a lead or two. Didn't he? He scratched his jaw with his good hand, thought about shaving, thought about going back to sleep, decided he wasn't sleepy anymore. Bone-tired, but not sleepy.

At least things were looking up. In the sense that he wasn't dead. His arm would heal. It was itching more than hurting right now, which had to mean he was out of the woods, right? The part of him that always cautioned him against optimism cautioned him against optimism. But it was hard not to feel he'd been through the worst and come out the other end.

Now it was just a matter of finding Amelia, and he had a promising start on that; then finding out what her connection was to Misty and the world of porn films, and reporting back to the old lady. Then maybe a vacation.

At his front door, he heard a knock. "Just a minute," he called. "Who is it?" And through the door, a friendly voice said, "Messenger service, Holland March home?" A glance through the peephole showed a guy with a genial smile standing there on the stoop.

"Hi," March said, opening the door, and Jackson Healy slugged him full in the face.

II.

Healy tore yesterday's page off his Word-a-Day calendar (*Vampiric*, adjective: tending to drain vitality, blood, or other resources), and looked at today's entry. He thought for a few moments, then said, "He responded to her vampiric drains on their bank account with equanimity." He smiled, pleased with himself, and went to make coffee.

Healy's place was small, quiet, empty. Spartan, you might say. That had been the word of the day a month back, and he'd saved the page, feeling it described him well.

On the TV, a newscaster was offering a smog alert—Stage Two, residents cautioned not to engage in any unnecessary exercise until after 6PM tonight, commuters encouraged to keep their windows rolled up on the drive home—and a glance out the window showed him why. A thick crust hung over Sunset Boulevard, and though the blazing sun was working hard to burn some of it away, it didn't seem to be making much headway.

Healy picked up a pinch of fish food, dropped some flakes onto the surface of his saltwater aquarium. The tank's two occupants swam toward the food, began nipping at it as it floated gently down.

The newscaster had moved on: "In other news, the police have not ruled out mechanical failure in the death of adult film star Misty Mountains, whose car plunged off the road in last Tuesday's…" Healy went to get dressed.

His closet held only a handful of clothes—half a dozen plain undershirts, a couple tropical-print button-downs, one blue leather jacket. He chose the next shirt in line and slid the jacket on over it. What was he forgetting? The address. He found the cow-shaped slip of paper with Amelia's writing on it, shoved it in his jacket pocket. Keys? Check. Hat? Nah. He flicked the light switch, turning out both the lights and the TV set, and out he went, locking up behind him. His brass knuckles gleamed dully from the top of the TV, where he'd left them.

Cruising up Laurel Canyon toward the address on the slip of paper, Healy noted the empty lawns, the lack of unnecessary exercise. Who wanted to be outside when the air was like this? Not that people did a lot of walking in L.A. even on those rare days when the smog was bearable. But a day like today? There was one young girl, maybe twelve, thirteen—just about Kitten's age, but this one looked like an actual child, not an aspiring hooker—walking along with an oversized book under one arm, and Healy thought back to his own grade school days. He'd never been much of a reader, but there'd been stickball and Indian wrestling and mumblety-peg with jackknives and plenty of other reasons to play outdoors. That had been in the Bronx, though, the Irish side, and they hadn't invented words like *smog* yet. You'd get beaten up going to the delicatessen and robbed coming back, but at least you could breathe the fucking air.

Healy drew to a stop at a traffic light just as it turned red. Watched idly as the girl approached a vacant lot between two houses, snaked under the chainlink fence that was supposed to keep it vacant, and carefully paced out ten steps this way, then six steps over, then three steps back, like she was following a treasure map. He half expected to see her break out a tiny shovel and start digging, but all she did was plop down on the ground, open the book, and begin reading aloud. Strange kid. Someone behind him honked then, and Healy noticed the light had changed. All right, you bastard, I'm moving.

Few minutes later, he found the address Amelia had given him and pulled over to the curb. It wasn't a fancy house—kind of run-down, actually, like whoever lived here hadn't put a lot of care into it. Not that Healy's own digs were fancy, but at least they were neat, orderly. Spartan.

Ah, well. He wasn't here to judge.

Walking up to the front door, Healy discovered he'd left his knucks home. For a second he thought about driving all the way back to get them, but that was idiotic. He could do this old-school for once. He made a couple of practice fists, cleared his throat, put on his game face, and rang the bell.

Holland March came to the door, unshaved, bleary, his left wrist swaddled in gauze, and Healy swung with a smile, confident the knucks would've been overkill. Maybe literally. You wanted to use the right tool for the job, and this fellow looked like a breeze could knock him down.

In any event, Healy's fist did.

He stepped inside, shut the door behind him, stood over March where he lay, crumpled, on the living room floor. Healy flexed his fingers, suddenly reminded that you wore brass knuckles not just to maximize damage but also to spare your own actual knuckles. But eh, he'd live.

"Mr. March," he said, in a measured and reasonable voice, "we're gonna play a game."

Give the man credit, he was struggling back up to his knees. "This is a mistake," he was saying, "I think you've got the wrong house—"

Healy kicked him, right in the breadbasket, and down he went once more, all the air driven out of him.

"The game's called 'Shut up, unless you're me.'"

March fought to get his breath back. "I…I *love* that game." He put one hand down on a low table, levered himself up.

Healy waited till March was standing again, then feinted with his left. When March raised his arms to block, Healy came in under with his right. *Oof*. And he was down again.

While March caught his breath, Healy looked at the pile of mail on the table. Bills, a catalogue or two. Frederick's of Hollywood, ha. He flipped open a kidskin wallet, glanced through the cards in their little plastic sleeves. Diner's Club, Red Cross—

Healy whistled low. He waved the wallet in March's direction. "You're a private investigator?"

March had managed to crawl over to the nearest wall and sit up, clutching his stomach. "Yeah."

"I've been thinking about it myself, sometime I might…"

"You'd be a natural," March said. "Look…there's just twenty bucks there. Take it."

"I'm a messenger," Healy said. "Not a thief."

"Wouldn't be stealing," March said. "I offered."

"Well, it wouldn't be right," Healy said, and put the wallet down again. He walked over to March, looking around at the room as he went. The place wasn't fancy, but it was nice enough on the inside. Some good furniture, looked solid, not that pressed-wood crap everyone was getting. Brass doodads on the walls. "You can afford to live like this, on a P.I.'s salary?"

"What salary?" March said, coughing. "I eat what I catch."

"You must catch pretty good."

March winced as he prodded his tender gut with his good hand. "It's a rental, okay? I didn't buy this stuff. We got it furnished. Till we're back in our place." Healy didn't say anything. "Yes, I can afford it. Some months." He hawked up some phlegm, spat. Looked up again. "So? What's the message?"

Healy crouched beside him, gave him his best stare. "Stop. Looking. For Amelia."

"I'm not even looking for Amelia! I'm, I'm on this case, she's just, like, a person of interest, man, she's not the one I'm—" Healy looked confused, and a little impatient. March saw Healy's hand start curling into a fist again. "Ah, fuck it. Message delivered. I'm done. Put a fork in me." He stopped. "Don't really put a fork in me."

Healy stood. "That's fine, Mr. March. Amelia's gonna be very happy to hear you got the message so quickly.

That's gonna make her smile, that's good." He cleared his throat. "Now. I got one more thing I need to ask you before we're done here."

March closed his eyes. He knew what was coming. "You wanna know who hired me to find her."

"That's right. Now we can do this easy way—"

"Her name's Glenn."

"—or we can do this the hard way—"

"My client's name is Lily Glenn. Two 'n's. Old lady, hired me a few days ago to look for her niece. Not Amelia, she's not the niece, it's this other woman, who's actually, you know, kind of…dead. Or maybe not, since the old lady says she saw her, alive, but I'm guessing she really is dead, 'cause the police say they have her body. But anything's possible, right? Anyway, that's who I'm looking for, and who I'm looking for her for. For."

Healy was speechless.

"Anything else…?" March spat again, saw some blood in it. Bet there'd be some when he peed too. He stood up, slowly, groaning all the way.

"You just gave up your client," Healy said.

"Well. I made a discretionary revelation…"

"No, you gave her up, just like that. I asked you one simple question and—" Healy made a chatterbox mouth with his hand and set it flapping. "You gave me all the information."

"I thought that's what you wanted."

"Some poor old woman pays you good money and that's how you treat her?"

March shrugged. There was a counter that separated

the living room from the pass-through kitchen and he leaned on it with both hands. Healy's eyes darted to the counter, but there were no weapons on it, not even a butter knife or something to throw, unless you counted the cookie jar. Which…it was ceramic, kind of heavy, better than nothing. Healy saw March casually slip his hand toward it. Desperate. Sad, really.

"*Ah…*" Healy said warningly, and raised one hand to block in case March tried throwing the thing at him. But March didn't throw it. He reached inside the cookie jar and came back out with a handgun: .38 special, wood grip, snub nosed. He swung it up, but Healy took him down with a lazy right cross to the jaw. He grabbed the gun out of March's hand as he fell, threw the thing into a corner. March landed on his ass by the wall again.

Healy bent down, grabbed him by the necktie, used it to slam March's head against the lower part of the counter. Yep, solid wood.

"Now, I'm very sorry that you didn't get the message," he said, and he really did sound sorry, probably because on some level he really was.

"Me too," March said. Everyone was sorry. "But I get it now. I get it, I dig it."

"Yeah?"

"Yeah," March said—and then went scuttling across the floor toward where the gun lay. Healy kicked it away just as March's fingertips brushed it. March let his eyes slide shut and banged his forehead gently against the floor.

"What about now?" Healy said. "You get the message now?"

"Yep," March said.

"Are you sure?"

"Yeah. I'm cool."

"All right," Healy said. "Give me your left arm."

"No!" March squeezed his arm tight against his side.

"Yeah, come on." Healy bent over him, wrenched his bandaged hand up behind his back. "You cut yourself?"

"I'm dealing with an injury!"

"Right, look," Healy said, "when you're talking to your doctor, just tell him you've got a spiral fracture of the left radius. Got that?"

"No, wait," March shouted, "wait, Jesus, man, stop!"

"Deep breath," Healy said.

March didn't take even a shallow one, he was too busy yammering, trying to talk Healy out of it. Ah, well. Some people just don't listen.

There was a loud crack and March screamed.

12.

Coming down the front steps, closing the door behind him, Healy saw the girl from the vacant lot coming the other way, toward him. She had a paper grocery sack in one hand, a bottle in the other.

They stopped, facing each other, at the curb.

The girl smiled. "Hi. Want a Yoo-hoo?" She held the bag up and Healy heard glass clink inside it.

"A Yoo-hoo?" He found himself smiling too. "Are you kidding?" He took a look in the bag, pulled one out. "Oh, yeah. You know, I haven't had one of those in about thirty years."

"You a friend of my dad's?"

"Yeah. Yeah, we're...business associates. He's inside. Resting." Healy shook the bottle hard. You had to mix a Yoo-hoo, he remembered, or you got the watery stuff at the top. "Hey, didn't I see you crawling around a vacant lot earlier?"

"Maybe?" the girl said. "I read there sometimes."

Healy nodded. He popped the cap, took a long swig. It went down smooth.

" 'It's Me-he for Yoo-hoo!,' " he said, then realized she wouldn't know what the hell he was talking about, having just been a baby when those ads were running. Hell, she might not even know who Yogi Berra was. Probably only knew the cartoon bear.

"Well," he said. "Thanks again."

The girl waved and walked past him to the door while he opened the door of his Chevelle. "Hey," he called back. "What's your name?"

"Holly March," the girl said.

"Holly and Holland. Cute."

"My dad wanted a boy," she said. "If I'd been a boy, I'd've been Holland junior."

"I'm sure he's glad with what he's got."

She shrugged. "Not usually."

Healy got in the car. He kind of wanted to say something more to her, like *Your dad's gonna be mad* or *You're gonna need to take care of him*. But he had a feeling she'd figure it out. Seemed like that sort of kid. Precocious.

He took another swallow and drove off.

Later that night, Healy could be seen lugging two colorful cartons down Sunset Boulevard, past the crowd lined up outside the Comedy Store, in through the public door at the front of the club, past the stage where some curly-haired comic was making jokes about gasohol, and then through the private door behind the stage that led to the stairs. As he lugged them, the cartons made the same clinking sound Holly March's grocery bag had made, and for the same reason. Yogi knew what he was talking about when he endorsed the stuff. And Healy was making up for decades of lost time.

Which, incidentally, was why he didn't drink anymore. Because he wasn't the sort of person who could take a taste and enjoy it and walk away. If he drank a teaspoon he drank a gallon, it was just the way he was wired. And a gallon of Yoo-hoo would just leave you hyper and pissing all night long, not in the *calabozo* with a shiner, bloody knuckles, and a judge saying, "Do you remember what you did, Mister Healy?"

Healy was preoccupied enough with these thoughts that he didn't notice, as he balanced the cartons on one hand and fit his key in the lock with the other, that someone from the club below had come up the stairs behind him. People did that from time to time, hunting for the bathroom, or maybe thinking there might be a better show playing on the second floor. Wishful thinking.

He half turned to look at the guy, an older man, black, horn-rimmed glasses, three-piece leisure suit. "It's not a public area up here."

The man nodded toward Healy's door. "What, you've got, like, an apartment up here?"

"If you're looking for the restroom, it's back down the—"

Suddenly his apartment door swung open. Another man stood in the doorway, younger, white, with brown feathered hair and aviator glasses and a black leather jacket. He had a gun in his hand. "We're looking for Amelia."

Behind him, the older guy pulled a gun, too, from the small of his back, a .38 very much like March's. Took his horn-rims off, tucked them away in a pocket.

"I don't know what you're talking about," Healy said.

"We'll see," the younger one said. And the gun swung up, came smashing down against the side of Healy's skull, dropping him like a stone.

Yoo-hoo bottles shattered on the ground.

13.

In this corner of Pasadena, the streets rolled up at night, and cars were mostly kept in garages. So Holly March felt awfully conspicuous sitting in the driver's seat of her dad's car at the curb outside the Leisure World retirement complex. Not least because she was twelve years old. Only until Thursday, it was true; after that she could at least say she was a teenager. But she had a feeling that "Actually, officer, I'm about to turn thirteen" wouldn't be much of a defense if she was challenged.

Not that age should be what mattered. She felt strongly about that. She knew grown-ups who shouldn't be trusted behind the wheel. Her dad, for instance. Not the most reliable of drivers, to say the least. And not in any condition to drive at the moment. What was he supposed to do, call taxis to take him everywhere? Hire a chauffeur like some Hollywood bigshot? With what money? Meanwhile, Holly knew all her turn signals, was careful and responsible, and her feet reached the pedals. What was the big deal?

She looked at her wristwatch. Mickey's big hand was pointing at the nine. How long did it take to say "I quit"?

When she'd gone into the house and found her father passed out on the floor, moaning softly, at first she'd thought it had been an accident. That nice man couldn't have done it—he'd drunk a Yoo-hoo with her. But when her dad finally came to, she got the whole story out of him. She'd made him swear he'd go straight to the client and drop the case, soon as they got out of the emergency room. He'd been more than willing. He should've never taken this case in the first place, he said.

But now he'd been in with the old lady for half an hour, and that didn't bode well. He was such a pushover, her dad. Couldn't say no to anyone. Especially when there was money involved.

"Do you really think she's still alive?" she'd asked him as they drove over here from the hospital.

"Who?"

" 'Who,' " she said. "The one she hired you to find. Her niece."

"No. The head medical examiner himself personally I.D.'d the body."

"Oh, I bet he did," she said.

"What does that mean?"

"I saw that picture you've been carrying around."

"You're not supposed to look at pictures like that," March said.

"Then don't leave them lying around the house."

"Touché," March said.

And after driving some more: "Dad?"

"What."

"Do all men like big ones like that?"

"Big what?"

" 'Big what.' " She rolled her eyes. "Boobs."

March stared straight ahead, out the windshield. "Yes," he finally said. "All men do."

Holly had nodded, filed the information away for future reference, kept driving.

Now she sat by the curb and picked at her fingernails. She checked her watch again. How much longer—

Then she saw him coming. His head was down, his shoulders slumped. The cast on his arm shone white as he passed under a streetlamp.

He climbed in beside her.

"Did you drop the case?" she asked.

"Sure, yeah," he said. "Case closed."

"Really?"

He didn't say anything. He'd meant to quit. He'd tried to quit. Then Lily Glenn had taken out her checkbook.

"Can I ask you a question?" March said. "Tell me the truth. And don't take it easy on me just because I'm your father. Just—tell it to me straight. Am I a bad person?"

What kind of question was that? "Yes," she said.

March sighed. "Just drive," he said.

14.

Healy slammed face-first into the wall, slid to the ground. The younger man, the one with the aviators and the jacket and the gun, loomed over him. Gold chains sparkled against his black-and-gold shirt, which he was wearing over a turtleneck. Guy was a fucking fashion plate.

In the background, the older guy was tossing the place. Which wasn't so difficult, because how much stuff did Healy have? A TV set, an aquarium, a calendar. Nine shirts in the closet, a few forks and knives and spoons. A can of fish food. The man was pulling out drawers, dumping the contents on the ground. Lots of luck. He wasn't going to find Amelia in there.

The younger one crouched next to Healy.

"I'm going to ask you again. Where is Amelia?"

Healy sat up. Spotted a cigarette pack lying on the floor where it had fallen out of one of the drawers. He reached for it, but the younger guy slapped it away.

From the club below, the sound of laughter wafted up. Applause.

Healy let out a breath. His chest hurt. "I would like to help you…but I just don't know anybody called Amelia."

The younger guy stood, casually, calmly. Then in one swift movement he drew back his leg and kicked Healy, hard, in the gut. Healy folded over sideways, retching.

More laughter from below, gales of it. Jesus, who'd they book tonight, Redd Foxx?

Healy forced himself upright again.

"You don't talk," the guy said, "I'm gonna have to start breaking your fingers." He let out a high-pitched giggle, like he was watching the show downstairs. "You understand?"

"I understand."

The older guy called out, his voice muffled because his head was in Healy's closet: "Hey, hotshot! Come on in here, I found something hidden in the cabinet."

The younger one crossed to the closet, came back carrying a heavy canvas duffel bag, dropped it on the table. Reached for the zipper.

"Oh," Healy said, "don't open that, that's not mine, it belongs to a friend, I just look after it for him."

The man's hand hung over the zipper pull. A smile creased his face.

"It's one of those bags," Healy said, "if you try to open it—"

But the man had already grabbed hold of the zipper and pulled it.

There was a loud splat as a cloud of blue paint erupted from the bag, covering the man's face and chest, his hair, his gold chains.

"Motherfucker!"

And with perfect timing, the nightclub audience below bellowed out its biggest roar of laughter yet. Like a sitcom soundtrack. Healy shook his head. "You know, that, um… that's not going to come off."

The guy snarled, savagely grabbed two fistfuls of Healy's shirts, rubbed them all over his face. Got them blue. Didn't get his face white.

He walked over to the aquarium, plunged his face into the water.

"Ah, Jesus, don't make the fish swim in that shit," Healy said.

The man pulled his head back out, flinging water all around him, just as blue as before.

"It's like one of those charges they put on the money in banks," Healy said. "It's supposed to be permanent. I tried to tell you."

Still dripping wet, the guy shouted. "You tried to tell me...?"

He reached into the tank, scooped up one of the fish, lifted it out and flung it across the room. It smacked the wall wetly. Fell to the floor.

"Oh, hey, come on, not the fish. Don't do that." Healy turned to the older man, tried appealing to him. "Can you please tell this guy to act like a professional?"

The older guy just shrugged.

Healy turned back to the younger guy, his voice suddenly serious. "You know, kid...when I get that gun off you, it's gonna be your dinner."

"Dinner?" The guy laughed hysterically, turned to his colleague. "This fucking man." The laughter ended abruptly. "You're funny. Dinner." He stuck his hand back in the tank.

"Don't," Healy said. "Don't."

"Come on, fish..." He grabbed the other fish, the

bright red one. He strode over in three furious steps, the fish squirming between his fingers. "You want some fucking dinner? You want some dinner? I got some dinner. Here you go. Eat that thing, you fucking fuck!" He threw it in Healy's lap.

Healy got to his feet. It was a slow process. His gut ached, his back, his head. He set the fish down gently on the nearby windowsill. "You've got to stop and think about this. All right? When you came here tonight, was this what you wanted to happen? What, you came here to make me eat some fish? To shoot me?"

He locked eyes with the man. Healy was slow to anger, but this guy had managed it.

"Look, if you come here, you beat up on me, you trash the place, I understand, I get it, it's part of the job, I accept it. I've done it." He shook his head. "But what did you do? You did something different from that, didn't you? You pissed me off. You made an enemy. Now even if I knew something, I wouldn't tell you, kid. You know why I wouldn't tell you?" While he was talking, he was edging toward the light switch. "And this is not my only reason. But it is a principal reason. No, I wouldn't tell you, because you're a fucking moron."

Healy's arm swept up, flicked the switch, and along with the floor lamp in the corner, the television set blared suddenly to life, volume up high. Startled, the two men spun, taking their eyes off Healy for a second, which was long enough for Healy to dive to one side.

The blue-faced kid swung back, arm up, aimed at where Healy had been standing beside the window. His finger was working faster than his brain, and by the time he realized Healy wasn't there anymore he'd already pulled the trigger. One of the windowpanes shattered—then another windowpane across the street, and a woman who'd been standing in the window went down with a yelp.

The older guy grabbed the younger one by the arm. "You stupid son of a bitch!"

There was screaming now across the street.

Healy, meanwhile, had hit the floor. Ignoring the pain in his side, he rolled under his table to the bed. He swept one arm under the boxspring and came up onto his knees with a double-action pump shotgun, primed and loaded and—

And the apartment door was swinging, the two men sprinting out.

Healy got off a shot, splintering the doorframe, but they were gone.

15.

It was Thursday, Holly's birthday, and the bowling alley had thankfully beaten out the beauty salon as the venue of choice. March could deal with a pack of adolescent girls in ugly shoes swinging bowling balls around. Nail polish remover gave him headaches.

Plus, they'd serve you a beer at the bowling alley.

But first the ugly shoes had to be dealt with. The girls were all calling out their shoe sizes at the same time, and the poor son of a bitch behind the counter didn't know where to start.

"Whoa, whoa, easy," March said, raising a hand. "Jesus Christ, one at a time, huh? *Thank* you. Now. Janet, size…?"

Instead of answering, Janet said, "You took the Lord's name in vain."

"No, I didn't," March said. "I found it useful. Cindy, you a six…?"

The rest of the afternoon was a blur. March nursed his injured arm, resting the cast on the side of the booth where he was also nursing his beer. The girls were squealing, laughing, cheering their little heads off. He could only imagine how excited they'd have been if they'd ever knocked down any pins.

The beer flowed, and the consequence followed, which is why March found himself on the toilet after the last frame of the last game had come and gone to a chorus of heartbroken "Awww"s and he'd only slightly reluctantly let himself be talked into paying for just one more. Let 'em enjoy themselves. Let 'em be twelve for one more day.

So he was sitting on the pot, cigarette between his lips, reading the cover story in the new issue of *Time* about the whole "Global Cooling" thing, which as far as he was concerned was up there with the killer bees and the Loch Ness Monster in terms of things to be scared of, but what the hell, it was something to read, when a pair of familiar-looking canvas sport shoes tromped into view outside the stall door and stopped, facing him.

A hand knocked at the door, once, twice.

"March? Jack Healy. Don't get upset, I'm not here to hurt you."

Just hearing that voice again made March's broken arm twinge. *Spiral fracture of the left radius…*

Healy went on: "I just want to ask you a question."

March swung the stall door open. By the time it swung wide enough to reveal Jackson Healy standing just beyond it, he had his gun out and pointed at him.

Healy didn't seem scared. Maybe the cast had something to do with that. Maybe it's just tough to scare someone when you're aiming at him from a toilet with your pants down around your ankles.

But you had to play the hand you were dealt.

"How stupid do you think I am?" March asked. "Huh…? I've got a license to carry, motherfucker. And ever since your little visit the other day…this little baby's gonna stay right *here*—" He gestured with his gun hand at his own chest, and the stall door started to swing shut. He banged it back open.

His cigarette, which had been hanging precariously, fell from his lips. It landed on his leg. He twitched wildly until it was dislodged onto the floor. The stall door started to swing shut again.

He banged it open once more. Started to get up, wrestling the magazine around in front of him with his bad hand to preserve his dignity, trying to pull his pants up with the same hand, cast be damned. And trying to keep the gun aimed at the same time. It wasn't working.

"Look away," March snapped, and Healy turned to face the wall.

"You know there's a mirror here, right?" Healy said.

"Close your eyes," March said. He wrestled with his pants some more. Fuck. "All right, you know what? Forget it. Turn around—"

"Can I open my eyes?"

"Yeah, open your eyes."

Healy did, saw March standing awkwardly in the door of the stall, pants still down, issue of *Time* clasped in front of his crotch, gun pointed crookedly at him

"What do you want?" March said.

Healy took a deep breath. Let it out slowly. He seemed embarrassed, and not just by March's pathetic situation, or his hairy knees.

"I, uh," he said. "I want you to find Amelia."

＊

They sat at a booth in the alley's diner, line of sight to where the girls were still playing gleefully. Healy was working on a slice of pecan pie while March stared at an untouched slice of the apple crumb, digesting a mug of coffee and the story he'd just heard.

"So you think these guys want to hurt this chick, Amelia?"

"Sure," Healy said between bites. "After they're done killing her." He finished off his ginger ale. They hadn't had Yoo-hoo. "You know, I asked around about you. A couple of people I trust say you're pretty good at this."

"Well, that's surprising, 'cause I thought your job ended with breaking my fucking arm."

"Well, technically it did. I'm off the clock. This is a separate situation. Trying to do some good, keep this girl from getting hurt."

March shook his head. "I'm not buying this nice-guy act, pal. She owes you money, doesn't she? You coming to collect? You want me to finger her so you can throw acid in her face…? Well, no. "

"No," Healy said, "she paid me up front, actually. I always get paid up front."

"Really?"

"Yeah," Healy said, "I used to let people pay after, or like half up front, half after, but this way really cuts down on problems."

"I'd think so." March thought about it. "Maybe I should try that." Sipped some more coffee.

"Yeah," Healy said. "Maybe."

They stared at each other.

"So what it is," Healy said, and then stopped, searching for words. What was it, really?

March just kept staring. Waiting.

"What it is for me, is…I like where I live. And I really don't want to have to move."

Healy dropped a wad of bills on the table, twenties and tens.

"Two days in advance. That's four hundred dollars. Plus whatever the old lady's giving you."

March exploded. "Old lady? Fuck *you*, old lady, you broke my arm, I *quit*, remember?" He looked Healy straight in the eye. "You said drop the case, I dropped the case." It was true enough, if you ignored the part where he let himself get talked into un-dropping it. Something he didn't much feel like mentioning, since he didn't want to have two broken arms.

But Healy floored him with what he said next. "So call her up, get back on the case. Get paid twice."

"Wow," March said. "That's how you operate? I mean… That is very telling. I'm a *detective*, and we have a *code*. We don't do that. But, interesting. That's the level you inhabit? Okay. Good to know."

"Then get paid once, I don't care. As long as you find her."

"Why do you even need me?" March asked. "You're the one who got money out of this chick. You telling me you can't find her again?"

"I never found her the first time. She found me. I give this course at the Learning Adjunct—"

March slapped his palm down on the table between them. He goggled at Healy. "No. You're not—holy Christ. I *thought* you looked familiar. You're the 'real-life tough guy'?"

Healy nodded uncomfortably.

"You teach courses in it! How to be tough."

"Just like self-defense, assertiveness…"

"And you need me—"

"Mr. March, you're a private eye. I'm not. And you were looking for Amelia already, right?"

"Well…yes and no."

Healy said, "Excuse me?"

"My profession's very complicated, okay? It's nuanced."

Maybe that was going to be one of his calendar's words sometime before the end of the year. But it hadn't come up yet. "What does that mean?" Healy asked.

March looked serious. "It's like there's mirrors inside mirrors."

"What the fuck are you talking about?"

"Remember I told you, this old lady hired me to find her niece, Misty Mountains?"

"Wait, Misty Mountains? The, the porno actress? The one who died?"

"The young lady," March corrected him. "The porno young lady. But yeah, she died in a crash, and then two days later her aunt goes to her house, to clean out the place, and lo and behold, alive and well: Misty Mountains. She sees her through the window. But when she knocks on the glass, goes to unlock the front door, she hears the back door opening, and by the time she gets around the house, the girl's climbing into a car. And zoom, off she goes. The girl, not the old lady. Misty."

"Bullshit."

"Bullshit's right. She's dead, then she's alive? That's what I'm talking about. It's very fucking complicated." March lit a cigarette. "But I persevere. You know? I work on it. And I think, maybe there *was* a girl there."

"Amelia."

March nodded.

"The old lady saw Amelia."

March made a 'bingo' gesture with one finger. "Look who decided to show up for class."

"So how did you get on Amelia's trail?"

March unfolded two more fingers.

"Three," Healy said. He frowned. "Three what?"

"Three days," March said. "In advance. If you want the rest."

"Fuck you. Come on? Six hundred dollars? That's fucking robbery."

"Yes, it is."

"I only got four hundred," Healy said.

"Well, it's early, you can go rob a bank if you hurry."

From right behind March came a *ba-dum-bum* and he swiveled his head, startled. Holly was there, perched at the corner of the booth. She hit invisible cymbals with an imaginary drumstick: *Tchh.*

"Jesus, what are you doing here?"

She sat down next to him. "Giving you a rim job," she said.

"Rim *shot*."

"Whatever. Hey, can we get one more game before…" Her voice trailed off as she noticed Healy there, sitting across from her dad, eating pie. "…You're the guy that beat up my dad."

"Hey," Healy said.

"No," March said, "sucker-punched your dad, big difference. But don't worry, he just did it for money."

"You beat people up…and charge money?" Holly asked.

March nodded. "Sad, isn't it, honey? How some people have to make a living?"

"That's really your job?" Holly said.

"Yeah," Healy said.

"Wow. So, um…how much would you charge to beat up my friend Janet?"

"How much you got?" Healy asked.

"Okay, this conversation is over," March said, shoving his plate over to his daughter. "Eat."

"We're just talking," Healy said.

"And it's over," March replied.

Healy leaned forward, tapped his fingers on the cash that was lying on the table. "Four hundred. That's all."

March thought about it. "Four hundred. Two days. We find her earlier, I still get to keep it."

"Done," Healy said.

"Great," March said. He scooped up the rest of the money, shot a glance at his watch. "Because I already know where she is."

16

The flyer didn't say *on* the air, it said *for* the air. It also said "for the birds," which March thought was probably the single stupidest thing you could say on a flyer if you wanted people to show up. But what did he know? The City Hall plaza was absolutely packed full of people, lying on the ground, and they'd all been drawn here by a promise that the time they were spending and the effort they were putting in was all for the birds.

There were some birds around too, pigeons, but with every square inch of pavement covered by one sprawled body or another, there was no place for them to land. They just circled around and then perched on a tree branch or window ledge or something. Served them right, fucking birds.

Walking over, March had tried to show Healy the flyer, explain how he'd gotten it from the bulletin board at the Iron Horse, talked to some people in the neighborhood about it after the bartender had chased him out, but Healy had been preoccupied with a newspaper he'd picked up from a bench they'd passed. The headline had caught his eye, and the photo beneath it.

" 'The late adult film star, Misty Mountains,' " he read out loud, " 'seen here at last month's Detroit Auto Show…' " He shook his head. "Kind of a high-profile case for you, isn't it?"

March snatched the paper out of Healy's hands, tossed it in the next trash can they passed. "You know, the thing about keeping your mouth closed is, it prevents speaking."

"Sure," Healy said. "Unless you're a ventriloquist."

They were coming around the side of City Hall. "Fuck those guys," March said. "You can always see their mouths moving."

"You can what?" Healy asked.

"Ventriloquism. Doesn't work."

"Sometimes it does."

"Never."

They passed a folding card table with a pile of gas masks on it, old military surplus stuff, and two girls behind it who looked like they were eighteen or nineteen and wished they'd been born long enough ago to be hippies. There was a stack of flyers, too, and one of the girls lifted two from the top and held them out to Healy and March. The other one said, "Welcome! Would you like masks…?"

Healy shook his head and they continued to the top of the steps. That was where they first saw the crowd. It had to be at least fifty people, all lying on the steps of the municipal building, arms and legs spread wide so that each person took up as much room as humanly possible. And, yes, they all had gas masks on. Because, you know, the air. The birds.

March took a long look at the crowd, at their hand-lettered placards and ratty khaki jackets with peace patches sewn on, at the handful of cops standing around on the perimeter wondering what they had done to pull this assignment, and turned to Healy with a smile. "All right. Well. Goodbye," he said.

"Hey, hold on," Healy said, "what do you mean, goodbye?"

"This is Amelia's protest group. Her crew. She's in there somewhere. So. Have at it."

He turned to leave.

"Wait," Healy said, "how do you know she's in there?"

"I'm telling you, this is her group. The people she introduced Rocco to. She started it."

"Okay, but if she's holed up somewhere right now, hiding, scared, what makes you think she's going to be here…?"

"Of course she's gonna be here," March said. "It's her protest group."

"Stop *saying* that."

"I'd like to stop saying that."

"I heard what you're saying, it's her protest group," Healy said, "but—"

"I don't hear you hearing me," March said. He walked up to the edge of the crowd, stopped with his feet just an inch away from the upturned soles of one protestor's Doc Martens. "Hey, Amelia?" he shouted. "Amelia?"

No response.

Healy joined in: "Amelia?"

Silence. It was at that point that March realized, for the first time, that the whole plaza was strangely quiet. No chanting, no shouts, no *Hey hey, ho ho*. What kind of protest was this?

"She's not here," Healy said.

"She's here." March raised his voice. "*Amelia*?"

Finally, from somewhere in the middle of the huddled pile of bodies, a voice answered. It was a woman's, high-pitched and muffled by the gas mask, but you could sort of make it out. "We can't talk to you."

"What?" March said. "Who said that?"

"We can't talk to you," came the voice. "We're dead."

"You're—" March dry-washed his face with his hand. He looked down at his shoes, started counting to ten. Gave up after four. "Yeah, okay, I get it. Very clever. I'm hip." He raised his voice again: "But this is actually a really serious matter."

"So is this," came the protestor's voice. "We've all been killed."

"No you haven't."

"Fuck you, man," came a second muffled voice, a man's. "We're dead."

A guy on the edge of the crowd smoking a hand-rolled cigarette leaned in toward March. He not only looked like Charles Nelson Reilly, he sounded like him too. "They can't talk to you, man. They're dead."

"Yeah," March said. "Thanks. That's helpful."

The smoker nodded, smiled. Healy asked him, "What's the protest about, do you know?"

The smoker took a long drag, then shouted, "Hey! Any of you know what you're protesting?"

The second protestor who'd spoken shouted back, "The air!"

"Air," said the smoker, taking another puff.

"You're protesting the air?" March said.

"The pollution!" the guy shouted back. "The birds can't breathe!"

"So you all died because of the pollution?" Healy asked.

A pause. "Right," came the voice.

"What about the gas masks?" Healy wanted to know. "They didn't save you?"

Longer pause. No one had an answer to that one.

Until someone did, a new voice, a low baritone. "They didn't work."

March waded into the crowd, trying not to step on anyone, but not trying too hard. "Can we get back to Amelia here?" He heard someone curse as he stepped on her hand. So sorry. "Look, Amelia?" He put both hands to his mouth, making a megaphone, though did that actually do anything? Did it make your voice any louder? Anyway, he did it. "We know you're here! We need to speak with you!"

Yet another protestor answered, another woman, sounded like a tenor. The four of them could've been a fucking gas mask barbershop quartet. "Hey, *dickhead*. She's not here."

"Of course she's here," March said. "This is her protest group."

March glanced back at Healy for help, but the big guy just shrugged.

"She's not here because of her boyfriend," came a new voice, and now it was a quintet.

"Her boyfriend," March said, turning toward the section of the crowd the new voice had come from. "Why?"

"Her boyfriend died. Like, really died. Three days ago."

"He died? Wait, then where is she?"

"Sorry, can't help you," the new voice said. "We're dead."

"Goddamn it." March looked up at the sky, found nothing he was seeking there. Just smog. So maybe these idiots had a point. But he really didn't much care.

"All right," he shouted. "Which one of you cock-and-balls wants to make twenty bucks?"

17.

They were in March's car. He was steering with his injured hand, his right resting by the controls for the radio and the cigarette lighter, and when the latter popped out, he used it to light a Camel. Healy was next to him, riding shotgun. In the back seat, one of the protestors had his gas mask pushed back on his head. His name was Chet. He looked about eighteen years old. He was twenty dollars wealthier than he had been when he got up in the morning, and he was directing them to their destination.

"Make a left here," he said, pointing, and March took the turn, drawing up to the sidewalk in front of…well, what would you call it? Not a house. Not anymore.

It looked like something a giant child might construct out of matchsticks. Burnt matchsticks.

They got out and—carefully—entered the structure. March knew a thing or two about home fires. Well, a thing, not two, but that was enough to know this had been an especially bad one. There was basically nothing left. No roof, no walls, just a few charred beams and the wreckage of some furnishings that wouldn't burn: the stove, the toilet.

"What the fuck is this, Chet?" Healy asked.

"Dean's house. Amelia's boyfriend. I told you, he burned to death." He looked around. "This place looks so much bigger now."

March said, "Did you even really know Amelia, Chet?"

"Yeah, well, kind of like, mainly through Dean?" He shrugged. "Dean was a filmmaker—I kind of like experimental kinds of films, that's kind of how we met, 'cause I'm kind of in the business myself."

"Yeah?" Healy said. "What do you do?"

"Projectionalist."

March and Healy exchanged a glance. They had the next George Lucas on their hands, clearly.

"Yeah, anyway," Chet went on, "Dean had like this whole room filled with film stock. One day it just went up—*whoof*. Cost the guy his life and his life's work. Kind of, I don't know, kind of makes you think, right?"

"Not really," March said.

Through the no-longer-a-wall fronting on the street, March saw a neighborhood kid bicycling past, a boy maybe fourteen years old with floppy hair down to his chin, skinny arms poking out of a sleeveless T. "Hey kid!" March called. "You know the guy who lived here?"

The kid braked his bike. "Maybe. What's it to you?"

Another tough guy. In a few years, he could take over teaching Healy's course.

Chet piped up: "He'll give you twenty bucks if you answer."

"Wait, I didn't say that," March objected, but the kid's eyes had lit up.

"Twenty bucks, man. Or you can blow."

March took a deep, deep breath. He was running low on cash, and it's not like he could get more today—the banks would close any minute. But he handed the kid a pair of tens.

"Thank you," the boy sang, cramming the money in his jeans. "Yeah, I knew the dude. Filmmaker dude. Saw him making a film last month."

Chet said, "Experimental film, right?"

"I guess… More like a nudie film."

"You see a girl about five-eight," March asked, "dark hair, named Amelia?"

He shook his head, hair flopping in his eyes. "Nope. Saw that famous chick, though."

"What famous chick?" Healy asked.

"The dead one. Porn star. Misty something."

"You saw Misty Mountains here?"

The kid nodded and grinned. He must've really *seen* Misty Mountains.

"But you didn't see this other girl, Amelia," March pressed.

"Nope," the kid said. "I hung out for a while, too. Talked to the producer. His name was Sid…uh, Sid Hatrack."

"Nobody's name is Hatrack," March said.

"Whatever," the kid said. "I tried to get a job. Offered to show my dick. 'Cause I got a big dick."

"Awright," March said, turning away. That was enough of that.

"That's very nice," Healy said. "You sure you didn't see another girl?"

"Nope," the kid said. "You guys want to see my dick?"

March said, "Nobody wants to see your dick, dude."

"Twenty bucks?"

"We already *paid* you twenty bucks," March began, then stopped himself. "What am I saying?"

"All right," the kid said, and began pedaling away. He called over his shoulder, "Fags!"

"Hey, kid," March called back.

"What?"

"What was the name of that film?"

"I don't know…" He thought hard. "Wait, yeah, I do. It was on the cans of film. Stupid title. *How Do You Like My Car, Big Boy?*"

18.

Night had fallen, and they were driving. March was at the wheel, and he was still fuming.

" 'Do you want to see my dick?' Unbelievable. This is what I'm talking about, it's over. The days of ladies and gentlemen are over, this is what Holly's looking down the barrel of. This is what she's dealing with, the fucking Chets of this world, and that idiot."

"Well," Healy said, trying once again to change the subject, "one thing we know for sure, something funny's going on."

"No there's not. Guy burned up. It happens," March said. "Trust me, I know."

"It happened three days ago, the exact same day Amelia fell off my radar."

March chuckled. "Your radar."

"Something's going on," Healy insisted. "And we're going to find out what."

March drove on, through darkness punctuated by grimy signs and grimier lives.

"Fine. You got me for two days. But two days is two days. That's the deal. Like it or lump it."

"Sure," Healy said. "Just to clarify—I decide to 'lump it,' what does that involve?"

"I don't know," March said. "It's from the Bible."

They turned onto Hollywood Boulevard, where the

signs were bigger, brighter, and advertised movies like *Jaws 2* and *Airport '77* rather than lube jobs and car washes. Nothing else changed much.

"Let me tell you what two days of detective work looks like," March said. "You drive around like an asshole. You're going to spend half the time interviewing guys like Chet, you spend the other half trying to translate from fuckhead-speak to English, and when it's over, the only thing that's changed is that the sun went down twice."

"And nothing ever works out, is that what you're trying to say?"

"Never."

"But you get paid," Healy said.

"Sometimes." March noticed something out of the corner of his eye. "Hey. Son of a bitch. Hatrack."

"What?" Healy asked, but March was already pulling over, coming to a stop at the foot of a giant billboard.

"Hatrack. Look."

Looming above them, lit like a thousand suns, was a sign topped by the words *A "Savage" Sid Shattuck Production*. At the bottom was the name of the movie, *Pornookio*, the letters all flesh-colored and the two middle Os sporting erect pink nipples. In between was a painting of a man with the red cheeks and long wooden nose of the puppet boy, only the nose was curved up like a giant dong and three women were straddling it. The one riding the tip, with just a sheet around her to cover her breasts, was Misty Mountains.

Healy said. "Sid Shattuck? Who's that?"

"Savage Sid, the porn king," March said. "Experimental

films, my ass. They were making a porno. And that kid
said Shattuck was there."

"Well, *he* didn't burn up," Healy said. "So let's go talk
to him."

March was on the phone, its cord stretching behind him
as he paced around the living room, while Holly prepared dinner: buttered toast and canned corned beef,
her specialty.

"I said I'd like to speak to Sid personally. I'm asking
after a friend of ours, Amelia. I'm an old friend. Yes."

Holly glanced through the front window. Healy was
waiting in the driveway, hands in his pockets.

"Why don't we invite him in?" she asked.

March covered the mouthpiece of the phone. "No animals in the house, sweetheart." He went back to his call.
"Yeah, I'm here. Say that again? Okay. Thank you very
much." He handed the receiver to Holly to hang up. She
dropped it on the sofa.

"Was that the number you got for Sid Shattuck?"

"Yeah," March said, grabbing his cigarettes and matches.
"They're getting ready for a party. I asked about Amelia,
and they said she'd be right back."

"Back? Like she's been staying there?"

"Yeah," March said, and struck a match. He touched it
to a Camel.

"So we found her!"

"Maybe." March shook out the match, went to the
closet, began strapping on his shoulder holster. "Can you
stay at one of your friends' tonight?"

"I can stay with Jessica, but…" She headed over to the stove, turned off the burners. Stuck the corned beef back in the cabinet. So much for dinner. "You're going to a party?"

"I'm going to a *big* party," March said. He was struggling to get the holster strap over his cast. She helped him with it. "Jacket?"

Holly dug his jacket out of a pile of clothes on the sofa. She looked unhappy.

"Sweetheart, it's a job. I've got to take it. If I don't, we won't get to live in such a nice house."

"I hate this house," Holly said. "We're not even supposed to be here."

"Go to Janet's."

"Jessica's."

Like he knew the difference. Wait, maybe he did. "Which one is she?"

"The one with brown hair."

March smiled. Brown hair. There was a distinctive feature. "She the one with the glass eye…?"

"The one that you like," Holly said, sort of disgusted.

"…and, like, the Hitler 'stache?"

Holly heaved a sigh, got her own jacket on, and walked out.

Near the front steps, she passed Healy. Right about where he'd drunk one of her Yoo-hoos before. She'd left the front door standing open, and he started toward it.

She watched him climb the steps, tried to think of something to say that would keep this evening from spiraling further out of control. "I'm friends with a cop, you know," she finally called out.

Healy stopped in the doorway. "Is that so?"

"He likes my dad a lot too."

"Maybe they should get married," Healy said.

Fuming, she turned and headed down to the street, where her father's car was parked.

This time, they were driving to Bel Air, and it might as well have been in a different state. Hell, it might as well have been on a different planet. No billboards dotted the landscape here, and no grime, either. Even the stars seemed to sparkle a little more brightly in the heavens, especially if you'd started the evening with a bump, as March figured most of Sid Shattuck's guests would have.

He, personally, didn't do that shit. You had to draw the line somewhere. But a drink never hurt, and he'd taken a bracing swallow before getting behind the wheel. He'd offered the pint to Healy, but the guy had declined, even after March had wiped the mouth of the bottle ostentatiously. And fuck, what difference did it make, it was alcohol, wasn't it, wouldn't that kill all the germs anyway?

But Healy had refused, and that had returned the evening to the sour note it had been on ever since they'd left the burned-out wreck of Dean's house.

They didn't talk most of the way, then Healy started grilling him. "So, you know…the old lady…did you believe her?"

"What about?"

"When she said she saw Misty alive that night. Did you believe her?"

"God, no. She's blind as a bat."

"Uh-huh."

"She has actual Coke bottles for glasses," March said. "You paint a mustache on a Volkswagen, she says, 'Boy, that Omar Sharif sure runs fast.'"

"But she read the license plate number off a moving car," Healy said. "And remembered it."

"What's your point?"

"The lady's not blind, and she's not crazy."

"And...?"

"I'm just saying, she saw something."

"Her dead niece, sitting at a desk in a blue pinstripe suit, writing her a letter."

"Something."

"You know, you're really getting on my nerves."

"I'm sorry," Healy said, "but I'm just saying—"

"Which one of us is the detective?" March said. "Which one? Okay. Okay. Because I was starting to wonder."

"I'm just saying—"

"Well, stop saying it."

"Because you don't want to hear it," Healy said.

"Because it's fucking crazy." March swerved around a hairpin curve, the sort he'd been navigating all night long, only brushing the guardrail a little, and fuck it, that's what it was there for, right? He screeched to a stop in front of Shattuck's house.

House, hell. Mansion didn't begin to do it justice. The place was huge, levels upon levels, not one but two pools in front, hot tub on the balcony, glass everywhere, lights everywhere. On a normal night it was probably just twice as big and garish as any of its neighbors, but with a party in full swing it was…beyond words.

There were people milling around on all those levels, and more inside, no doubt—at least a hundred, maybe more, and easily enough clothing to cover twenty or thirty of them. An R&B group was laying down a smooth groove on a stage by the trees, some Earth, Wind & Fire tribute, and then March realized it *was* Earth, Wind & Fire.

As he got out of the car and handed the keys to the valet standing by the entry gate, a man walked by, leading a horse that had been dressed up to look like a unicorn, pointy horn bobbing on its forehead.

"Jesus tap-dancing Christ," March said.

19

Unlike March, Healy wasn't a California native. He wasn't even a New York native, technically, since he'd been born aboard a U.S. military transport ship halfway across the Atlantic Ocean. Long story. But he'd settled with his mother and brother in the Riverdale section of the Bronx before his first birthday, and he stayed there until his eighteenth, and if you'd asked him then whether he'd ever move to the West Coast, he wouldn't even have said no, he'd just have laughed, and then maybe decked you for good measure.

But the judge had offered him a choice: probation or jail. And probation meant The Program, and The Program meant California. If his father had been around, maybe that would've changed things, or maybe it wouldn't, but anyway the old man was still stationed in Germany then, batting cleanup a dozen years after the fact.

So—it was California or bust.

He'd done two stints on a fruit orchard in Heritage Valley, picking lemons and oranges and avocados in the summer sun, back-breaking work that had built up his muscles and stamina, taught him enough Spanish to get into a fight but not out of one, and more than once made him wish he'd chosen jail instead.

That was college for Jackson Healy. That was how he spent years nineteen through twenty-one, and when he was finally finished, he swore (among other things) that he'd never eat a fucking avocado again. And he never had.

Why hadn't he moved back east afterwards, when he had the chance? He'd learned the word for that from his Word-a-Day calendar too: inertia. It meant the tendency of an object at rest to remain at rest or an object in motion to remain in motion, which had confused him at first—how could the same word mean both that you can't move and that you can't stop moving? It was like a Thermos bottle, keeps hot food hot also but keeps cold food cold. What if you put an ice cube in one and boiling hot coffee in another? Why does that work? But the point became clearer when he thought about it this way: you keep doing what you're already doing. You stay where you are and what you are. You wear the clothes that you've already got in your closet.

So what clothes were in his closet? California tough-guy clothes. Jackson Healy learned the art of persuasion from guys his size who'd been doing it all their lives, and he started doing it too, first as the backup guy on a two-man team, then on his own. He'd put on a few pounds since then, but you know what, that actually worked to his advantage. He wasn't a fucking schlub, he still had muscle under there, but people tended to run away less when the guy knocking at the door looked a little softer around the edges.

And that was Jackson Healy's story. He'd become a heavy, in both senses, and maybe that's all he was ever meant to become. His big brother had become an Air

Force engineer, chip off the old block, and speaking of the old block, his father had come back stateside and gotten himself stationed in San Diego, where in theory Healy could've seen more of him, maybe brushed off that old relationship and started over, but then there was the whole thing with June and his dad, and, well, that had been the end of that. Inertia. You keep doing what you're doing, and the sun goes up and the sun goes down, just like March said. Nothing changes.

But then one day? You get out of a car and a man walks a fucking unicorn across your path.

A unicorn.

And the guy by your side is a private detective, a bit of an asshole, it's true, and a bit of an idiot, but, you know, also kind of a nice guy, and he gets to work in this world while you're beating up deadbeats and cradle-robbers. In the city you've lived in almost your entire life now, just over the hill and down the highway, there are unicorns. And you think to yourself, well, Jack, maybe once in a very long while there's something new under the sun after all.

20.

"All I told him," the girl in the red dress was saying, "was if you want me to do that, then don't eat the asparagus!"

The blonde next to her, in a green shift that hugged the curves of her breasts, seemed puzzled. Asparagus? What?

Healy seemed to be fascinated by them, poor guy probably hadn't seen girls this hot ever, outside of a movie, but March, frankly, was just trying to get his car parked. He'd handed his keys to the valet, was waiting for the goddamn chit in return, but the guy was staring at the trunk of his car for some reason.

Wait. Okay. That was the reason, something was banging around in it.

He walked over to the car, stared at it. *Bang, bang. Bang.* There was someone in the trunk. Hammering to be let out.

He unlocked it, and saw Holly staring up at him, looking sheepish.

"I know what you're going to say," she began, and damn right she did, "but since I'm already here, you might as well take me in with you, right?"

She peered up at him hopefully.

March slammed the trunk shut again.

He walked over to the valet, keys extended.

"Um, I can't take your car like that," the guy said.

March pivoted on his heel and returned to his car.

❄

Holly struggled as he led her by one arm toward a rank of taxis standing near the entrance. "Stop it," she muttered, and dragged her arm free. People were looking. "Stop it, dad!"

He grabbed her arm again, dragged her onward.

She couldn't believe she'd gotten so close and was about to be sent home, missing not just a chance to stay near her dad and maybe protect him a little, but also the biggest party of her entire life. Jessica would be *so* jealous. And Janet—Janet's head would just explode.

She stared at the women swarming around the bar, the ones clutching silver purses under one arm while sipping from martini glasses, the ones laughing by the side of the pool. Some looked like movie stars. Some looked like what they were.

"Dad! There's like whores here and stuff."

"Sweetheart," March said, "how many times have I told you, don't say 'and stuff.' Just say, 'Dad, there are whores here.'"

"Well, there's, like, a ton," Holly said. Her dad swung open the door of a waiting taxi and shoved her into the back seat. "Wait! No! I can help you! Seriously? I came all this way—"

"I love you," March said and slammed the door shut. He patted the taxi on the rear, like patting a horse on its flank, and off it went, Holly glaring at him through the window.

Well, that was a good start to the evening.

He collected Healy and they walked in together.

❄

Earth, Wind & Fire was singing *"Do you remember…"* which was kind of ironic, 'cause March didn't figure half the people here would remember a thing about tonight when they woke up in the morning. Everyone was trashed, high, on something or other. On one bench they passed, a group of girls was laughing uproariously as one jammed her hand up another's skirt, emerging a few seconds later from the girl's cleavage clutching a coke spoon. Hilarious. On the other side, a skinny little runt with strings tied to his arms and legs and rouge on his cheeks was sporting an Alpine hat and Pornookio schnozz. "It's not my nose that grows!" he crowed at anyone who would listen.

March recoiled, shuddering, and almost collided with a stilt walker covered in leaves and branches. "What are you supposed to be?" he found himself asking.

"A tree."

They walked on. Shattuck had to be here somewhere— it was his house. But finding him, that would be a challenge. Not least of all because they didn't know what he looked like. Talk about a needle in a haystack. This was like a needle in a stack of needles.

Speaking of which, yep—the mermaid sitting with her tail in the pool was shooting up.

"Hoo," Healy said, waving one hand in front of his face, "well, we know Mary Jane turned up."

"What was that?" March said.

"Mary Jane. Marijuana. Pot."

"Yeah, probably," March said.

"Place *reeks* of it," Healy said.

"Oh, yeah," March said. "I can't smell."

"You what?"

"I can't smell," March said. "I got hit in the head a while back, I lost my sense of smell."

"You…can't smell."

"Yeah."

"You're a detective who can't smell?"

"Yeah."

"Oh, this just keeps getting better and better."

"Wow," March said. "That's really insensitive." But Healy had already walked away. He jogged to catch up.

They passed through an open sliding door and into the house itself. The crowd in here was dense, wall-to-wall sideburns and shellacked hair. You couldn't walk two feet without brushing up against some girl by accident. It was like a bouncy castle for grown-ups.

"Look," March said, "if Amelia doesn't show, we've still got Shattuck. But if we start asking questions and things get rough…" He raised his cast. "I'm injured. So you're gonna have to handle it."

"I think," Healy said, "this is going to work better and faster if we split up."

"What?"

"If you see a guy with a blue face," Healy said, "you come and find me." And he backed away into the crowd.

March was on his own.

He turned and pushed his way to the bar. There was a cocktail waitress there wearing a headpiece made of cigarettes. He snagged one, jammed it between his lips. Fine. Leave me here with one fucking arm to face off against who knew what. He raised two fingers, caught the bartender's attention. Courage might not come in a bottle, but what did was the next best thing.

Healy, meanwhile, was making his way down a corridor that led past a billiard room on one side and a projection room on the other. A man wearing a furry White Rabbit head from *Alice in Wonderland* came by in the opposite direction, a couple of tarts in French maid outfits on his arms. A girl balancing a tray on one hand extended a bright yellow cocktail in Healy's direction and wouldn't take no for an answer when he tried to refuse it. So he ended up with a drink in his hand for the first time in… how long? A long time. He sniffed at it, was relieved to find it smelled repulsive, and set the glass down on the nearest empty surface he could find.

"Hey!" The voice sounded more amused than upset, and looking down Healy saw it belonged to a woman covered from head to toe in gold body paint who was bent double, hands and feet on the floor. Healy's glass was sitting on her lower back, where a skimpy G-string disappeared into the crack of her gold-painted ass.

"Sorry," he said, picking up the glass.

"That's okay," the woman said, smiling at him, upside-down.

He set the glass down again, on a wooden cornerpiece this time. It was wonderland, all right, and everything was topsy-turvy, and somewhere in the middle of all this craziness was a frightened girl who'd paid for his help.

That's what he had to remember. None of the rest of this mattered. It was just a distraction.

Healy made his way to a padded door, quilted fabric cushioning the surface. There was no knob. Healy pushed it in, was greeted by the sight of the fanciest bathroom he'd ever seen, marble floor and Jacuzzi tub and gold fixtures and a girl with both palms braced against the edge of the sink, taking it from a man who looked like Don Rickles. Healy backed out quietly, not that either of them had noticed him.

Onward. A second door hid a broom closet. But then the third—

Healy stepped inside and slid the door shut behind him. He was in a dim, narrow passage with posters from various Sid Shattuck productions on the walls. After a bit the room widened and Healy could see racks of clothing, stacks of empty film cans, piles of props. It was a storage room, full of the detritus of moviemaking, and Healy couldn't help wondering if this is what Dean's place had looked like before the fire.

Healy lifted the cans one by one, looking at the titles. *Pornookio* was there, and *Alice in Nookieland*—Healy was beginning to detect a theme—and *The Opening of Misty Mountains* and *Pretty Passion* and *The Contempt*. One can was labeled *Misty, Test Footage, Reel 1* and contained a couple of slides, a few strips of film, and a little slip of paper Healy recognized, not because of what was written on it—

28-10 Burbank Apt
West, Flt D, 10:30pm

—but because the slip of paper was pink and shaped like a cow.

Amelia had been here. He pocketed the note.

None of the cans said anything about cars or big boys. But the costume racks were a different story. The metal bars were hung with plastic-bagged suits and dresses and lingerie labeled in Magic Marker with the name of the performer and the production, and on the second rack he checked, Healy struck gold. *How Do You Like My Car, Big Boy?* asked one card after another, and below that *Juliet* or *Blair* or *Sean*.

Or *Misty*.

Healy pulled down one particular *Misty* bag, gave it a closer inspection. A costume like any other. Tacky, not very well made, nothing about it that would make you give it a second glance if you saw it in a secondhand store. But Healy gave it a second glance and a third before hanging it back where he'd found it. It was a royal blue suit with white pinstripes.

21.

At the bar, March drained his third glass and was feeling pretty courageous. He wagged a finger at the bartender for another.

"…it's the killer bees," he said, as the man poured. His voice didn't sound slurred to him. "That's what you've got to worry about."

The bartender took this advice in stride, as he'd been taking the advice of drunks in stride for the better part of thirty years.

March tossed back the drink, then turned to a platform beside the bar where a painted go-go dancer was shaking her perfect breasts and absolutely no one was paying attention. He almost felt bad for her. "Excuse me…?" She bent down. God, those really were perfect.

"Hello, handsome," she said.

"You uh, you seem to have a very good vantage point up there," March said. "I lost my, uh, sister. She's got dark hair, your height…she's wearing clothes, but… Answers to Amelia?"

"Hey," the bartender said. "Why dontcha leave the girl alone?" He filled March's glass again. "Have another drink."

And so it went, the better part of the evening fading into a blur as March alternated drinks and questions,

questions and drinks. There were several bars in the place, and March found them all. He sampled concoctions he'd never tried before, didn't even ask their names. Girly drinks with twists of lemon peel, bright red drinks and aquamarine ones stinking of Curaçao, drinks in rocks tumblers and drinks in flutes—if someone handed it to him, he drank it. Well, why not? It was part of the job. Blending in.

"Hi everyone," he said to a group of women at one bar, the least crowded of them, one that fronted on a thick glass window into a swimming pool, behind which two bare-chested girls in mermaid tails were swimming around, occasionally nuzzling each other. How did they stay down there, he wondered. Maybe they're actual mermaids? He tried to collect his thoughts. "I'm Amelia…she's about…" He raised his hand to clavicle height. "…dark hair…and answers to…" One of the mermaids was waving at him through the glass. He smiled. "…the call of the wild? Just kidding, I forgot her name. But, you know, if you see you, just, if you see, let me know. And, um, tell me my name."

The women stared at him, puzzled, before turning back to their conversation.

"All right, then," he said. He wondered what Healy was doing at this moment. The poor guy. He meant well, March knew that, but he couldn't possibly be making as much progress as March was.

22.

What Healy was doing at that moment was passing the window of the projection room, on his way back to the main area of the party to find March. But what he saw through the window stopped him. Not the Sid Shattuck porno film currently being projected on the wall of the room, he was a big boy, he'd seen his share, but the audience sitting there in the room watching the film: a fat bearded guy in a blue T-shirt and some sort of elaborate headband, a woman with long, straight blonde hair and a deep scoop-neck shirt showing off her two scoops, and a thirteen-year-old girl sitting beside them, taking it all in avidly.

Holly.

Healy went in, placed himself between the projector and the wall, tried to ignore the sex act playing out on his stomach. "Holly, hey…I don't think you should be watching this."

The fat man butted in. "What's it to you, idiot? Move. You're in the way."

Healy grabbed a fistful of hair without even looking, bounced the man's face off the glass coffee table in front of him. The glass spiderwebbed from the impact.

"Listen, dickweed, that little girl is a minor. Where do you get off showing her stuff like this anyway?"

"He's not showing it to me," Holly protested.

"He isn't?" Healy looked over at the guy, who was now cradling a bloody nose.

"No," Holly said, and nodded to the woman next to her. "She put it on."

Healy looked over at her. What was she, all of nineteen? Twenty? "Yeah, well, she shouldn't be watching stuff like this either."

"Watching it?" the woman said. "Man, I'm *in* it."

Healy stepped out of the path of the projector beam, took a closer look as the image landed on the wall again, large as life. Ah. Well, there you go. He just hadn't recognized her with her mouth full.

"Right." He turned back to Holly. "Look, go home. Your dad told you to go home, go home."

She was staring daggers at him as he made his way out of the room.

Composing herself, feigning nonchalance, she turned back to the blonde beside her. "Men," she said, and her new friend nodded in total agreement.

"Hey, by the way," Holly said, "I'm supposed to meet someone here. Do you by any chance know a girl named Amelia?"

The blonde thought about it. "She in the business?"

"I think she did a film with Sid Shattuck," Holly said.

The blonde shook her head. "Don't know her. But if she's a friend of yours, tell her to stay away from Sid. He's gross." She leaned in conspiratorially. "He told me this one chick was his sister, right? Then a few days later, I walk in on them and they're all, doing anal and stuff!"

Holly favored her with a superior smile. "Don't say 'and stuff,'" she said. "Just say 'They were doing anal.'"

Now it was Healy's turn to go from bar to bar, looking for March. He didn't find him. At one bar he might have, if he'd been looking up rather than down as the mermaids behind the glass swam past and a man in boxer shorts and a wifebeater with a cast on one arm swam after them, in hot pursuit.

But Healy was looking down at that moment, staring at the cow-shaped slip of paper he'd retrieved from the storage room, trying to make sense of Amelia's cryptic notes. Flt D—Flight D? Burbank Airport? Was she flying somewhere at 10:30PM? What day?

He pocketed it again and looked up, but it was too late, March was gone. Healy asked the bartender if he knew where Sid Shattuck was.

"The guy who owns the place? Haven't seen him."

"How about a girl named Amelia, about so tall, dark hair—"

"Jesus, is everyone looking for that chick? I already told your friend, no, I don't know her."

"My friend—was he a guy with a blue face…?"

The bartender looked like he'd finally lost his patience. "No, guy with a cast on his arm. His face was the usual color. Now, are you drinking anything or just keeping me from serving other guests?"

Healy gave him a tight smile, nodded his thanks, moved on.

°

Outside, on the deck—one of Shattuck's many decks—March was doing his best to wring out his sopping undershirt and wondering whether the water might have damaged his cast. It hadn't been worth it. The mermaids hadn't known anything.

At least the weather was nice and the view was spectacular, a clear night sky twinkling away above them and the vast bowl of the L.A. cityscape twinkling away below. Immediately beneath the waist-high railing surrounding the pool was a steep grassy hill leading down to a patch of woods and then the fence at the edge of the property. March leaned against the railing and lit one of the cigarettes he'd left on a lounge chair before going for his swim. His clothes were still there, and what was more remarkable, so was his gun in its holster. Sometimes your faith in your fellow man got rewarded.

Now, how was he going to get that holster on single-handed? Literally single-handed. He'd never thought about that expression before, but he thought about it now. Why do people with two perfectly good hands say they're doing something single-handed when they're not?

He pondered this for a bit, felt his brain clicking along nicely, not so fuzzy anymore. The night air was sobering him up. That was something, anyway.

He smoked his cig down, pitched the glowing butt over the railing, watched it fall. Then went to get dressed.

"Hey," a woman's voice called as he laboriously twisted and pulled his way into the holster strap. She was wearing a beaded and fringed bikini top and a full-on Indian head-dress, though under the outfit she looked like a California girl through and through.

"Hey," March said. "Want to help me out with this?"

She came over, helped him buckle the thing on, got him into his white leather jacket. "You always packing?"

"Sure," he said, picking up the drink he'd left by the pool, "I'm a cowboy. And you…?"

"Pocahontas," she said, coyly.

"What do you do?"

Another coy smile. "I do a little acting."

"Me, too," March said. "Go like this." He made a gun with his thumb and forefinger.

"Okay," the girl said.

"Now shoot me."

"Huh?"

"Shoot me shoot me shoot me," March said. "Fucking shoot me."

The girl went *bang bang* with her finger and March fell back, one hand to his chest. "Ah! Got me!" He laughed. "Pretty good."

She did it again. *Bang!*

"Oh! Ah!" March reeled toward the railing, smiling. He felt the wood against his hip, reached out for it with his hand, felt nothing under his palm but air, and then he was tipping backward, his feet were coming up, and holy fucking shit, he was going over.

He hit the ground hard, the steep grassy hill, and tumbled ass over teakettle all the way down, smashing against rocks and roots and turning full flips in midair. He was so startled he didn't even try to hug his broken arm to his torso, or his unbroken arm for that matter, or tuck his head. He just bounced like a rag doll until gravity pitched him up against the trunk of a tree with an impact that drove all the air out of his chest. He was wheezing, trying to fill his lungs.

Up at the railing, the girl in the Indian war bonnet clapped merrily. "Woo! That was great!" Then she walked off to find someone else to talk to.

23.

Miraculously, March didn't seem to have broken anything else—not even the glass he'd been holding when he went over, though the drink in it had vanished somewhere along the way. He set it down on the grass, felt his body to make sure all vital parts were present and accounted for. They were—but his holster was empty.

"Shit!" he shouted. "Shit! My gun—"

He went down on all fours, pawing the grass, searching for his missing firearm.

Behind a nearby tree, a flicker of movement startled him. A woman in a canary-yellow dress peeked out from behind a branch. "Jesus," he said, "you scared me."

The woman didn't say anything. She had brown hair, was about so high—

March squinted. "Do I know you?"

She looked frightened.

"I'm not here to hurt you," he said, getting to his feet again, palms extended placatingly. "I'm just looking for my gun."

She bolted, racing away from him through the trees as fast as she could go.

Had that been…?

He took a few steps in her direction, hit something with his foot, bent down. His gun. "I got it!" he shouted, but she was long gone.

He checked the gun for damage—as well as he could in the darkness—and slid it into his holster. Then he sat back against the nearest tree, cracked out a battered cigarette from his jacket pocket, and lit it.

Something at the edge of his vision caught his eye, something revealed in the flickering flame. He turned to get a better look.

A dead body stared back at him—or would have stared if it hadn't been missing half its face. What should've been a staring eye, albeit a dead one, was a bloody exit wound, the remnants of a gunshot to the back of the head. It looked like raw steak. March felt bile coming up his throat.

The guy had on a frilly tuxedo shirt. He had a little spade beard, like a college professor. And half his head was blown away.

March found himself hyperventilating.

Why? Why did these things happen to him?

Why couldn't Healy have found the dead body instead? Speaking of the devil—

From the balcony he'd pitched headfirst off, he heard a familiar voice calling his name. "March? March?"

Healy, god bless him, it was Healy. But he sounded so very far away.

March tried to muster the strength to call back to him. "Hhh…"

That was all that came out. He tried again: "Hhhh…."

He felt like Costello in an old Abbott and Costello movie, trying to tell Abbott he'd just seen a ghost, or Boris Karloff or whatever. "Hhh…Hee…Heeeallly!"

"March?" Healy was up by the pool, and he ran over to the railing now, peered over into the darkness.

March got to his feet somehow. "Healy! Come on! Come down here!" He didn't like the pleading note in his voice, but sometimes you just couldn't worry about such things, and this was definitely one of those times.

Healy looked down at him. "What the fuck are you doing down there?"

"Get down here!"

Healy took a more careful route, climbing over the railing where the lawn was walkable, and slowly walking it. When he got to the tree, March jabbed an arm toward its roots, which were lost in shadow.

"What?" Healy wanted to know.

March just pointed again, and Healy took a closer look. "Fuck…"

"I'm going to be sick now," March said.

Healy went over to the body. "Who the fuck is that?" He clearly didn't much want to do it, but there was no alternative. He pawed through the dead man's jacket, coming up at last with his wallet. A Master Charge card told him who the fuck it was.

"That's Sid Shattuck," he said.

March squeezed his eyes shut. "Don't tell me that. Oh no. *Shit.*" He pounded a fist against his leg. Which, you know, hurt. He made a mental note not to do that again.

"What's going on here?" Healy said. "Everyone who worked on this Amelia flick…the boyfriend, and Misty, now Sid…they're all dead."

"Before we go solving the crime of the century," March said, "let's deal with the fucking rotting corpse!"

"What do you mean?"

"We've got to get rid of him," March said.

"Why?"

"I lost my gun, there was a girl, she can place me—"

"Right," Healy said. Looked around. His eyes settled on the fence. "I've got a plan. You throw up, then we'll get rid of the body."

March went to a tree and threw up.

Upstairs, Holly was wandering the corridors of Sid Shattuck's mansion, poking her nose in here and there. She'd already seen some things she knew her friends would never believe, and she was looking forward to regaling them, but what she hadn't seen any sign of was Amelia. She also hadn't seen any sign of her dad, thank goodness, or of Healy since the projection room, but how long could her luck hold out?

She squeezed past a woman who was saying, "I know, right?" to a man who was weighing her breasts on the palms of his hands, and made her way down the hallway outside. One more wing of the house and then she'd have been everywhere—

A figure loomed up before her, a woman who gave the impression of being twice Holly's height, and only some of that was due to her impressive platform shoes. When she spoke, it was in a posh British accent that reminded Holly of her mom. If this amazon's height hadn't been enough to intimidate her by itself, that would've sealed the deal.

"Hey," the amazon said.

"Uh, hi."

"Are you the one who's been asking about Amelia?" the amazon said.

"I, uh, may have said something," Holly said.

"What do you want with her?"

What would dad say, what would dad say—

"She's my sister," Holly said, "see, and yeah…I need to warn her. These two freaky guys were coming around, they were all like, 'Where is she, where is she?' It scared me, kind of." She swallowed hard. Playing scared wasn't so awfully difficult right at this moment.

The amazon scrutinized her and appeared to reach a decision. "You seem like a decent kid. I'll take you to her."

Holly gave a nervous nod and an uncertain smile, and followed the amazon toward the front door.

Healy had pulled the short straw and was carrying Sid Shattuck by the shoulders, one hand lodged in each of his armpits. The ruined head lolled against him, leaving bloodstains on his shirt. March had Shattuck's knees in his hands and was standing between them, walking backward. He was urging Healy to go faster.

"What I can't figure out," Healy said, "is how you saw him, from all the way up there."

"Come on, just go," March said.

"You didn't fall down the fucking hill, did you?"

March just grunted, kept moving toward the fence.

"Did you fall down the hill? Are you fucking drunk?"

"I had two, three drinks, tops."

"Yeah, that's why you can't walk straight."

"Oh, excuse me. I'm carrying a dead body and I have his schvantz in my face, I'm sorry I'm not Bakishnirov—"

"You can't even say 'Baryshnikov.'" They were at the fence, and Healy laid down his end of the load, leaving March holding Shattuck's legs up in the air by himself. "You did, didn't you? You fell down the fucking hill. You get drunk, you lose your gun, you take a header off the balcony, and now you're gonna tell me it's like a, a hallowed, time-honored detective ploy, right?"

"It was very slippery up there, okay? I was in the pool, I—"

"You were *in the pool*?"

March dropped Sid's legs. "Yeah."

"Why?"

"I had to question the mermaids. What were *you* doing while I was working?"

Healy was speechless. Couldn't think of a goddamn thing to say.

"Thank you," March said.

"Let's get rid of this guy," Healy muttered.

When they had Shattuck aloft again, they carried him right up to the fence at the edge of his property. Over the side he'd go, and then he'd be someone else's problem. With any luck, he'd lie undetected under a tree for a good long time. Hell, maybe the neighbors were out of town; maybe they never came to this remote corner of their property; maybe he'd never be found.

With any luck.

On the count of three, they pushed him up and over

the top. Waited to hear him land with a thud on the other side.

He landed—but not with a thud. Instead, they heard the sound of smashing glass and splintering wood and shattering plates and tumbling cutlery. And screams—lots of screams.

Peeking over the fence, they saw Shattuck lying sprawled on the wreckage of a long dinner table, with one, two, three, four, five, six people seated around it in fancy dinner wear. Well, not seated. Not anymore. And was that…a bride?

Healy and March pulled their heads back to their side of the fence and fucking ran for it.

"Hop in back, sweetie," the amazon said, and opened the door to a stretch limo idling in the driveway.

Holly wasn't sure this was the best idea. Why would Amelia be in a limousine? But she didn't know what else to do. So she climbed in. "This one says she's Amelia's sister," the amazon said to someone inside. Then the door shut behind Holly with a click.

Her eyes took a moment to adjust, but even before they did, she knew she was in trouble. There was only one person in the car with her, and it wasn't Amelia. It was a man, not a woman. And as he leaned forward, she saw that his face was stained a vivid shade of blue.

24.

The blue-faced man clapped his hands together and giggled in a way that was deeply disturbing. "Is that a fact? Her sister," he said softly. "Good times."

"I…there's someone out, looking for me," Holly said.

"Really," the man said.

She fumbled with the door, trying to get it open. He leaned over, pushed her hands away. "Hey, hey, don't touch that." He waved a long index finger in her face. "You just sit back and get comfortable. We're gonna have a little talk. Sis."

If she had been able to open the door again, she might have glimpsed her father at last, and Healy too, since they were both walking as swiftly as they could along a second-floor landing toward the stairs to the driveway. Before they reached the stairs, Healy got waylaid by the blonde from the projection room who wanted to know why he hadn't stayed to watch the rest of her movie. March didn't stop. He needed to be out of there, somewhere far away, far from dead bodies and grassy hills and crazy people. Healy would catch up. Or if not, he could take care of himself. He wasn't the one with a broken arm.

March raced down the stairs, looked around for the valet, spotted him, then felt around in his pockets for the parking chit. Oh, please. Don't let it be back on the hill…

He found it, dug it out.

Healy, meanwhile, had dislodged himself from the conversation with the blonde and was hastening to catch up. In his haste, he shoulder-checked a guy in a crimson three-piece suit coming the other way. "Sorry," he said, barely noticing the other man. But the other man noticed him.

"Hey," the man said—and then his face hardened. He reached behind him, to the small of his back.

That was when Healy recognized him: the older guy, from his apartment—the black guy with the horn-rimmed glasses, though he wasn't wearing them now, the one who'd escaped just ahead of Healy's shotgun blast. The one working with Blue Face.

The one with a .38 in his hand.

Someone in the crowd screamed as Healy grabbed the guy's arm and the gun went off, the bullet caroming off a railing overhead. More people screamed as they really got into it, Healy landing a solid punch on the guy's midsection. What he wouldn't have given for his brass knuckles now. The man may have been older, but his gut was like a fucking rock. They wrestled for the gun and it went off again, taking down a passing waiter.

March looked back over his shoulder from the foot of the stairs as the first few screams escalated into a full-on panic, people climbing over each other to get the hell out of the path of the bullets.

He saw Healy grappling with the other man near the hot tub while the people in the tub leaped out of the water like seals at the zoo, one man sporting a shiny pair of bikini briefs and another nothing but an erection.

Jesus. March was so glad he'd sent Holly home. He was a good father.

Was he a good detective, though? That was his client up there, possibly fighting for his life. He had an obligation to him, or maybe he did, March honestly couldn't remember all that much of his licensing exam, and his sense of ethics was squashy. He kind of thought maybe he should go help, but... Broken arm. That's got to be a free pass, right?

And Healy was a big guy, he could handle himself. March waved for the valet.

At that moment, Healy wasn't handling himself so much as being handled. The older guy had an iron grip to go with his gut of steel, and he was using it to force Healy's head back, one palm pressed against Healy's chin. Healy bit down hard, getting a mouthful of fingers, and the man howled in pain. They swung around, grappling, and struck the rim of the hot tub. The gun went off again, and this time the bullet went over the side and straight into the shoulder of the stilt walker, who fell like a chopped-down redwood.

Healy strained to turn the other man's hand, slowly angling the gun back toward him. If he could get it pointed at him and squeeze the guy's finger on the trigger—

But the guy was having none of it. He landed a barrage of punches on Healy's face that left him reeling. The guy got his gun hand free, aimed at Healy. In desperation, Healy swatted at the gun and it went flying, right into the hot tub, where it sank to the bottom.

Healy kicked out brutally, catching the older guy in

the belly and sending him stumbling back toward the
stairs. But the guy was a pro and recovered in an instant.
He slipped a hand into his pants pocket and came out
with a switchblade that opened with a flick of his wrist.
The long blade gleamed under the deck lights.

Healy whipped off his jacket, wrapped it around his
arm, and waited in a crouch by the hot tub. The guy came
forward, blade swinging, his stare merciless. Healy met
him forearm-to-forearm as the knife came down. He tried
to land a punch or two before the guy could get the blade
free for another swing, but the guy was fast. The blade
slashed, cutting through the jacket and drawing blood.
Healy shoved him off. "Fuck!"

Which happened to be exactly the word escaping
March's lips at that instant, as he watched, neck craned,
from the driveway below, his escape halted halfway to the
valet's station. He kept repeating it to himself—"Fuck,
fuck, fuck"—as he stupidly turned and ran back toward
the stairs.

Who the fuck was Healy to him, that he'd put himself
in danger to help him? Huh?

But there he was, racing for the stairs while everyone
else was still pouring down the other direction, trying to get
away. He could sit down and have a good long think about
it later, but right now, he was gonna fucking get up there.

In the back of the limo, Holly was terrified.

In another thirteen-year-old that might have produced
paralysis, but she'd been fending for herself for some
time now and wasn't about to let some blue-faced psycho

take her for a ride without a fight. She reached for the door handle again.

"I need to go right now," she said, firmly, and when the guy tried to pull her hand off the door, she shoved him back, hard. "Get *away* from me," she shouted, and scrambled for the door. This time she managed to get it unlatched before he lunged at her.

The door swung open, and through it they both saw the valet at his station, and next to him a scared-looking brunette in a canary-yellow dress. "I need my car, I need my car," she was saying. "Hurry!"

Under their blue lids, the guy's eyes lit with recognition. He shoved Holly back against the seat with one arm, held her there while he leveled a gun out the door with the other. "Don't fucking move," he growled at her.

He sighted, his finger tightened on the trigger.

Holly fucking moved. She reached under his arm for the door handle, and swung the door shut on his hand. She heard bones crunch as the gun went off, the shot missing the girl and shattering the valet's key stand instead. A hundred car keys jangled to the ground in a heap.

"Fuck! Motherfucker! My fucking hand!"

Holly didn't wait around to hear more. She tumbled out of the car shouting, "Amelia! Run!"

March heard the gun go off, turned back to look, saw the girl from the woods—yellow dress, brown hair, it was Amelia, of course it was, fuck—and behind her, another girl, younger, smaller, slimmer, go racing after. They vanished down the slope of a hill leading to the highway.

The younger one had looked familiar, too, somehow.

No, wait. It couldn't be. That was impossible—

"Holly? *Holly*!" Fuck Healy. He put his head down and barreled back through the crowd, whacking people aside with his elbows, with the cast, with his shoulders, he didn't fucking care, that was his goddamn *daughter* out there. He wasn't a detective anymore, he wasn't even a father, he was a goddamn guided missile. March had already lost one of the only two women he'd ever loved, he was damned if he was going to lose the other.

He whipped past the valet, who pointed at the departing taillights of the limo as it tore off down the road. "Hey, man," the valet called, "that girl in your trunk? She was in that car. With the guy who was shooting."

March nodded as he ran. Car. He needed his car. He needed *a* car. Now. At the foot of the driveway, a man was climbing into the driver's seat of his red Camaro, and then he wasn't, he was sprawled on the pavement, and March was climbing in, tearing off after the limo.

Up by the hot tub, Healy had the situation under control in the sense that he wasn't bleeding to death. But not in any other sense. He *was* bleeding, for one thing, even if no major arteries had been nicked, and the man who'd made him bleed was still at it, swinging that goddamn switchblade around like a refugee from *West Side Story*, only with less dancing and finger-snaps and Lenny Bernstein on the soundtrack.

Healy ran at him, caught the other man's arm with his, and squeezed tight, trying to break his grip, but no dice.

He'd lose if he ever arm-wrestled this guy. Brute force wasn't going to win the day. Healy glanced around for anything he might be able to use to his advantage. There wasn't much out here. The hot tub, the lights mounted on the walls. Some overturned furniture, none of it within reach.

The knife was slowly inching down toward Healy's face. With a grunt, he bent his knees, tightened his hold on the man's arm, and pivoted. They spun, winding up against the hot tub again, Healy's back painfully pressed into a corner of the power box that brought electricity to the whole set-up.

The power box?

Healy grabbed the other man's wrist in both hands and wrenched it forward, toward him. This caught the man off guard and he overbalanced. It was just enough of a lapse to give Healy the chance to squeeze to one side and jam the point of the knife blade deep into the guts of the power box.

A fury of sparks exploded and the man was literally blown off his feet, landing flat on his back two yards away, the knife sailing out of sight behind him. Healy had escaped the brunt of the charge, but he'd gotten some of it. He fell against the tub and held onto the rim, breathing hard, trying to clear his fried brain. His hair felt like it was standing up.

And you know what else was standing up? Behind him, he heard the guy standing up, too.

What the hell? What did it take to stop this son of a bitch? He tried to turn to face him, but he was too slow.

The guy was on him, steel grip at the back of his neck, forcing his face down toward the still-swirling water of the hot tub.

Healy tried to fight back, struggled to keep his face up, but he was forced down into the water. His lungs instantly started aching. On a good day, maybe he could hold his breath for half a minute. And this was not a good day.

He whipped his arms back, elbowed the man in the ribs, forced his head up above the surface, gasping for breath. Then the bastard had shoved him in again, and he was drowning.

He looked around in desperation. Water, water everywhere. There was a poem that went like that, wasn't there? He half remembered it from grade school in the Bronx, being made to recite it while Billy Mehl behind him kept sticking him with the point of a pencil, the little bastard. Funny, the things you remember at a time like this. Water, water everywhere—

But there wasn't water everywhere. There was something else down here too, along with all that water, and Healy reached for it, strained to get his fingers around it. At first he thought he wouldn't be able to, and then he felt it in his hand, closed his trembling fingers around it, and pulled the trigger.

The bullet exploded out of the .38, punched through the side of the hot tub, and blasted a hole the size of a small lemon in the older guy's leg. Water gushed through one of these holes, blood from the other. The guy fell back, letting go of Healy's neck, and Healy roared to his feet, gun in his hand, his face flushed, water spraying everywhere. He wanted to sit down and just breathe for an hour two, just enjoy the beautiful sensation of air going in and out of his lungs, but what he did instead was barge forward and slug the guy once, twice, again, pummeling him in the face with the gun until he went down.

Healy dropped to his knees beside him, gave him another for good measure. The guy's face was a bloody mess—not quite as bad as Shattuck's, but nothing you'd want to take a picture of and send home to mom. But Healy didn't feel an ounce of remorse. The bastard had tried to kill him.

The guy was saying something, mumbling as Healy raised his fist once more for a knockout blow. The guy lifted his hands weakly. "No…please…my leg…"

Healy hesitated. Looked down at the guy's leg. It wasn't gushing anymore, but it sure didn't look pleasant.

The man was trying to sit up.

"I swear to god," Healy said, leveling the gun at him, "you get up, I'll shoot you in the cock." The man lay back down again.

"I can…I can pay you," the man whispered through his mangled lips.

"You trying to *negotiate* with me?"

"You'll never see me again…"

Healy thought about it. This one was a pro, unlike his blue-faced friend, who was just a goddamn psycho. Pros he could work with. "Where you gonna be?"

"Michigan."

Healy stood. "Michigan works."

He tossed the man's gun back in the hot tub, grabbed his jacket from where it had fallen. The sleeve was pretty much ruined, he could throw the whole thing in the garbage. One more thing to chalk up to this fucker's account. But what the hell. He could buy a new jacket. The guy would have to buy new teeth.

Healy looked over the edge of the balcony as he slipped the jacket on. Down past the driveway with the milling, agitated crowd, past the hill and the highway curving around it, he saw two figures running, two women. They sprinted over the asphalt and under the glare of the magnesium lights. Healy squinted. Holy shit—he knew both of those women. And the cars squealing around the bend in pursuit? It looked like a black town car and, a quarter mile behind, a red Camaro. One of them might be March. But the other—

Healy turned and ran back through the house. No way he could catch up following on foot. But if he took a shortcut through the woods where they found Shattuck…

Maybe. Maybe he wasn't too fucking late.

25.

Holly had Amelia's hand in hers as they ran. The girl was barefoot, Holly didn't understand how she could keep running, her feet must be bloody by now, but she didn't question it, just kept trying to put more distance between them and the limo. If they could make it into the trees...

But two girls on foot are no match for a 180-horsepower engine, and they were still in the middle of the road when the black Cadillac came tearing around the curve. It squealed to a stop on the shoulder and the back door opened. They were caught like deer in the proverbial headlights, only the headlights weren't proverbial, they were real, and so was the gun in the blue-faced guy's hand.

Suddenly they heard the sound of another car engine, loud and getting louder, and the gunman spun to face it. Holly pulled Amelia by the hand and they hared off into the trees, running blindly toward the next bend in the road. If they could flag someone down, another driver, anyone—they might just possibly survive this.

Behind them, Holly heard gunshots split the night, but the bullets didn't seem to be hitting anything near them, so she just kept her head down and ran.

⸺

What the bullets had hit were the front windshield of the car her dad had stolen, and then the driver's-side door and the trunk as the Camaro had skidded past the gunman on its way toward a fucking enormous tree. The front bumper crumpled like a gum wrapper and March took the steering wheel right in the sternum, his forehead banging down for a glancing blow. "Ow," he said, blinking to clear his vision. He was seeing double—two gunmen racing down into the trees after his daughter, two Healys scrambling out of the woods on the other side of the highway and down the steep incline to where March was.

Two Healys?

March raised an unsteady hand toward the figures in the cracked windshield. "Hey…"

"You okay?" the Healys said, in unison. Their outlines were moving together and apart, together and apart. Right now they looked like Siamese twins. "Car still go?" the Healys wanted to know. March shrugged. "Stop fucking around! Come on!" The Healys didn't wait, they just ran off into the woods.

Well, good, at least that evened the sides up a bit. Two gunmen, two Healys. Two girls. Fuck. The Healys were right, what was he just sitting there for?

March threw the car into reverse and stomped on the accelerator. The engine burned, trying to pull away from the tree. He groaned with frustration, fed more gas to the engine, and tried not to think the worst when he heard the loud bang in the distance below. Come *on*. Finally the car took off, and as he drove, for the first time in a long time, March started praying.

o

What March had heard had not been a gunshot, though it could have been one and very nearly was. The blue-faced gunman had emerged from the woods thirty feet away from where Holly was holding Amelia up with one arm around the waist and trying to flag down a passing car with the other. She'd had no success. And now—the gunman laughed to himself—now she never would.

He paced slowly toward them, gun dangling down by his side. He wasn't in any rush now.

"Freeze!" he shouted, but it was a joke, 'cause they were already frozen, right? Like little bunny rabbits, like the ones he'd first learned to shoot with, god almighty had his brother squealed when he'd found 'em all dead by the well, but hey, little bro, that's what animals were for, wasn't it? You killed 'em, you skinned 'em, you ate 'em, you didn't fucking cry over them, boo hoo, like a little girl. He'd never managed to toughen the boy up, thought for a while maybe he was one of them switch-hitters like you saw on TV sometimes, but no, the prick was married now, four kids, so he must've learned to put it in sometime, but fuck almighty, the boy had been a pussy growing up. Anyhoo—

"Wow," he said, "you guys are *fast*! Woo!" He laughed loudly. Then he raised the gun. Enough. Time to get paid and back to Detroit and his cover job as co-head respon-sible for Troop 782. *We're loyal to purpose and integrity/ Pledged to the Scout oath eternally...*

His finger found the trigger, stroked it gently, then started to pull.

The girl, the younger one, looked really anxious now, which was how he liked it, but weirdly she wasn't looking at the gun. They always looked at the gun, especially little girls. But this one was looking up over his shoulder, and she was saying something: "There's a—"

He whipped around, just in time to see the front grill of a speeding van from two inches away.

Then he was lifted off his feet and slammed through the air, his jaw and shoulder pulverized, his gun hand snapped backward so the knuckles lay flat against his wrist, his pelvis fractured in five places. He felt blood filling his pants, his socks, his chest. And then for just an instant he felt the road under his back. He didn't feel anything else from the neck down after that, because his spine had snapped.

The van pulled to a stop a few yards down. The girls ran up to it, waving, hoping to get in, but seeing the heap lying in the middle of the road, the driver just shouted, "Holy shit!" and tore off. Leaving Holly and Amelia shivering and alone in the darkness. Well, almost darkness— the road was dotted with lights here and there, and there was one not too far away from where they were standing. And almost alone. The heap in front of them was still breathing.

Holly started to go to him, but Amelia held her back. "What the hell are you doing?"

"He's hurt!" Holly shook her arm free, started toward the gunman again.

"Are you crazy?" Amelia said. "Get away from him!"

"Just hang on. We need to help him."

Amelia watched as Holly gingerly approached the fallen man, but only for a few seconds. Then she turned tail and ran, vanishing into the trees.

Holly knelt down, took the injured man's hand. You could still see traces of the blue paint, even under all the blood. His hand was shaking. She tried to steady it. "It's okay," she whispered. "You're going to be all right. I'll— I'll get help." She realized that she was crying. For what? For this man who'd tried to kill her? Who *would* have killed her for sure? But the next word came out of her throat all the same, and she meant it as much as she'd ever meant anything she'd said in her thirteen years: "Sorry."

Healy burst out of the woods. "Holly?" He saw her then, saw the man on the ground, saw the man's tangled, broken limbs, heard Holly crying.

"A car hit him," Holly called, her voice ragged. "We need an ambulance!"

Healy jogged to her side. "Go see if you can flag somebody down." He looked at the gunman, who was looking back up at him. The man's eyes were open. Healy watched him blink, watched him breathe. "He's in a bad way."

Holly stared, the way a kid might stare at roadkill, which of course was exactly what this was. She was horrified, fascinated, repelled. "Go," he said.

She took off down the road.

Healy waited till she was out of sight beyond the curve, then crouched beside the fallen man.

A wheezing breath. "You…"

"Yeah, me."

The gunman somehow managed to laugh. He coughed, and the spittle that flew from his mouth was flecked with red. "You ever," the man said, his voice barely more than a whisper, "hear of John-Boy?"

Healy shook his head, no.

"By now…he's heard of you." The man's eyes held his, pain warring with satisfaction in them. "They're flying him in," he wheezed. "Now he's going to kill that private cop, and his whole fucking family." Another laugh shook the man's broken chest. "And then he's going to come for you. You ain't got long to live."

"Well, buddy," Healy said, folding a handkerchief he'd taken from his jacket pocket, "none of us do."

He reached down with the handkerchief in his hand, took hold of the man's neck.

Now, Jackson Healy's grip might not have won him an arm-wrestling contest with this boy's partner, up by the hot tub, but he'd spent summers picking avocados, and oranges, and lemons, and in all the years since he hadn't exactly become soft. And a man's trachea isn't much stronger than an avocado. It doesn't take all that much force to collapse it, no, not even with a lovely layer of blue paint covering it.

Healy squeezed and wrenched and watched the light go out of the man's eyes.

Holly ran back, arms and legs flying. You haven't seen anyone out of breath until you've seen a thirteen-year-old girl, heartbroken and terrified, gasping in the middle of a highway in the middle of the night. "Healy!" she shouted, when she'd gulped enough air in her to manage it. "There's no one here!"

Then her gaze fell to the man on the macadam, saw that he wasn't moving anymore.

Healy said, "He didn't make it."

Holly stared at him, a question in her young eyes, which maybe didn't look quite so young anymore.

She didn't ask it.

Behind her, the busted Camaro raced around the curve and skidded to a halt. March climbed out of it and Holly ran to him, fell into his arms, was enveloped in a hug. She was still a little girl, she was; maybe not for much longer, but right now, that's exactly what she was.

"Are you okay?" March asked.

"Yeah."

Over his daughter's shoulder, March exchanged a glance with Healy. In the air they both heard sirens. They were far away. They were getting closer.

"And that'll be the cops," Healy said.

26.

The red-and-blue flashers were still going, casting their glow over the scene, but the sirens thankfully had been silenced. The cops at work were pretty much silent as well, bagging the body, wheeling it in through the rear doors of the ambulance, cleaning the blood off the pavement as best they could once their photographer and the forensics guys had gotten what they needed. Everyone kept their heads down. Nobody recognized March. He'd been out too long at this point.

The lowly patrolman who'd been assigned to babysitting duty looked apologetic, but he had his instructions.

"Look," March said, lighting his last Camel, "you already got our statements, can I go see my daughter now?"

"Sir, I was told to keep you here so I'm keeping you here. Just following orders."

March was losing patience. "You know who else was just following orders? Hitler."

Healy looked at him, almost said something, then decided it wasn't worth it.

March threw up his hands, kicked at the ground with one toe. You had to show some backbone at times like this, not just stand there and take it. He didn't understand how Healy could look so relaxed, so calm, like a stubbled Buddha, like there was nothing he'd rather be doing than waiting to be questioned again. Some tough guy.

March aimed a finger at the cop and was about to let loose with a proper tirade when the most beautiful woman he'd seen all night walked briskly over. She was wearing a tailored yellow blazer over a cream blouse and delicious café au lait skin. She also wore a clipped, professional expression. She nodded to the cop: "Officer." Then she turned to Healy and March. He let his finger drop.

"You're Mr. March, I think? And you are…" She gave Healy a closer look, and a smile cracked through her professional veneer. "Hey, I know you. You're the, uh, guy, the diner guy, right? From last year?"

March gave a double take, stared from the woman to Healy and back again. You might generously have described Healy's expression as a smile, but March knew a wince when he saw one.

"Yeah," Healy said, less Buddha-like now. He seemed embarrassed about the whole thing. But what was the whole thing?

The woman nodded. "My name is Tally. If you'll follow me, my boss would like a word." She extended one arm toward an unmarked car idling by the side of the road. Tinted windows, government issue. "Please."

They followed her.

March said, sidelong to Healy: "I'm sorry, the 'diner guy'?"

"I'll tell you later," Healy said. March kept staring at him. "Don't worry about it."

They reached the car. Tally knocked on the rear door, and the tinted window rolled down. Behind it, sitting in the back seat, was a blonde woman, middle-aged but still pretty damn sexy, dressed in a severe ecru business suit that only made her sexier. At the moment she looked tense, like she had things on her mind other than boning a one-armed private investigator, so March kept his private thoughts to himself, put on a serious expression of his own, or the nearest thing he had.

The woman spoke stiffly, through narrowed lips, as though the necessity for even one sentence of small talk pained her. "How do you do?"

March glanced around at the scene. "About this good, most of the time."

"My name is Judith Kuttner," the woman said. "I work for the Department of Justice."

She let that sink in for a beat, and it sank, but it didn't hit bottom. So? March hadn't figured she was from the Department of Agriculture. He shrugged. "Okay, well, that explains…basically nothing."

The woman's eyes slid shut for a moment, and March thought she seemed to be struggling to maintain her composure. She apparently won the struggle, since when she opened them again, the no-nonsense look was back.

"I'm Amelia's mother," she said.

27.

In the outer office, Tally was entertaining Holly with card tricks, or trying to. Holly wasn't your average thirteen-year-old and Tally's attempts were landing on barren soil.

"Holly? Are you still frowning? What's in my hand?" She made a five of clubs appear out of thin air. "Ah?"

Holly said, "I know how you do that."

She had her work cut out for her, March knew. But then so did her boss, if she was going to bring them up to speed on a case that just got murkier and more confusing the more they looked at it.

Kuttner was sitting behind an impressively large wooden desk in her inner office, with an American flag standing beside it and leather-bound volumes of legal rulings or something like that arranged on a wooden bookshelf against the back wall. All of which added up to her being someone pretty high up in the organization. They didn't issue desks and flags like that to just anyone.

"First of all, I want to say thank you," Kuttner began, her voice still showing a good deal of emotional strain, but not quite as frosty as it had been at the crime scene. "We've been watching all the interviews, and it sounds like you might have saved my daughter's life."

"That was mostly Holly," Healy said. "His daughter."

March shrugged. "It's genetics."

Seeming to feel she had to make a gesture of some sort,

Kuttner pointed to a glass bowl on the corner of her desk. "Would you like a mint?"

March glanced at Healy, saw the man nod, and grabbed a sloppy handful.

And that was all in the way of social niceties this woman was capable of. She got down to business. "I need your help. But the situation is very serious, very delicate. I need to know if I can trust you."

Healy said, "I'm kind of getting the idea that, you know, you might not have much choice."

"Well, all the same, I need to know. My job can be very public sometimes. My office's role in certain high-profile cases means I have to be careful about who I associate with."

"Hey," Healy said, snapping his fingers, "that's where I know you from! The TV. You're prosecuting that, that car company thing."

Kuttner nodded, looking only slightly more comfortable than Healy had when Tally had remembered him from the diner. "The lawsuit for the catalytic converter, yes. Litigating against the auto companies to address air pollution. That's half my day. The other half I spend on pornography."

March lit up. He didn't know fuck-all about catalytic whatevers, but this was in his wheelhouse. "Oh yeah? What kind? Like which films? What's your favorite?"

Healy shook his head, muttered to him, "No, no—*anti*, um," he laughed uncomfortably, glancing in Kuttner's direction, where she sat sporting a humorless expression, "*anti* porn."

"Right," March said. He nodded and tried to look like that's what he'd meant all along.

"Like a crusader," Healy said.

March nodded some more. "Should I be writing this down?"

Healy said, "Yeah, write it down." March grabbed a pen from a set on the desk, found a scrap of paper.

"The Vegas Mob is trying to spread its porn operation to Hollywood Boulevard," Kuttner said, and March made a noise with his tongue that he hoped sounded disapproving. "And I'm doing everything I can to stop it."

"Thank you," March said, nodding earnestly. His pen moved, and he mouthed the words as he wrote them: "Porn…is…bad…"

Healy jumped in. "Wait, something I don't understand. Your daughter, she did a film with Sid Shattuck—"

"She didn't *do* a film, Mr. Healy, she wrote and co-produced a film, and her friend directed it. That's not quite the same thing."

"As what, fucking on camera? No, I suppose it isn't. All the same," Healy said, throwing Kuttner's words back at her, "if her mom's this anti-porn crusader…I just wonder, why would she do that, when she knows that's just gonna be extremely professionally embarrassing to you?"

Kuttner sighed. "Because she wanted it to. She wanted to embarrass me. She lashes out. We have a difficult relationship."

March nodded, sympathetically this time. His arsenal of nods was getting a real workout tonight: earnest, sympathetic. "Mothers and daughters, it's tough."

Kuttner just stared at him.

"All right," Healy prompted, "so there's this film out there."

"No," Kuttner said, "there's no film anymore. There was a fire. This friend of Amelia's I mentioned—"

"Dean," Healy said, and Kuttner looked surprised. "Yeah," Healy explained, "we went to his house—well, what's left of his house."

"He was apparently editing the film when the fire started," she said. "All the footage burned. Everything."

"Yeah," Healy said. "And Dean with it."

"Mrs. Kuttner?" March leaned toward her. "Why do you think everyone involved with this film is dying?"

"I have no idea, Mr. March. I wish I did. I only know that Amelia's in danger."

"Why don't you put her in protective custody?" Healy asked. "I mean, after tonight she's probably very scared, she might want to be at home…"

"She doesn't trust me," Kuttner said. A painful admission, apparently. "She thinks of me as the government, and she doesn't trust the government. She thinks I'm *behind* all of this. Somewhere she's out there, and she won't call home because she thinks her mother is going to have her killed." Jesus, was she tearing up? This tough broad?

Healy dug his handkerchief out of his jacket pocket. "Here, want to use that?" They all looked at it, the blood-stains glaring under the office fluorescents.

"No, thank you." Kuttner reached into her desk drawer

and took out a checkbook. She opened it on her lap, uncapped a pen. "I want to hire you both. Please: find her. Protect her."

March sat back in his chair. Now they were getting somewhere, and it was somewhere he liked. "Okay," he said, "you can hire us, but we're not cheap. This is very intensive work, and for something like this I'd say…"

Kuttner had already started to write out the check.

"…we couldn't do it for less than five thousand dollars," March said.

Her pen hung above the checkbook.

He nodded. Determinedly.

She looked down into her lap, at what she'd already written there, out of sight of the detectives. To: *March Investigations*, Amount: *Ten Thous*

"Okay," she said. She ripped out the check, tore it in half and then in half again, started writing out another.

March threw a wink in Healy's direction. Stick with me, professor. I can teach you a lesson or two myself.

When it was dry, Kuttner handed over the five-thousand-dollar check. March pocketed it, then looked back over his shoulder at the outer office. Holly was sitting quietly, Tally across from her, smiling broadly. God, that smile.

March reached toward a business card holder on Kuttner's desk, picked out one of her cards. "Can I take this?"

"Fine," Kuttner said. She sounded eager to have them out of her office.

"Does, uh, Tally have one?" March asked, casually. Or

anyway he'd meant it to sound casual. "Should we have hers as well? Just in case you're not, uh, around? You know, if we need to get in touch with somebody…?"

Kuttner's glare could've cut glass.

"That's okay," March said, "I'll just ask her."

"Mrs. Kuttner," Healy said, "one thing we could use, actually, is a photo of your daughter. I see you have one there—" He nodded toward a metal frame with a snap-shot of Amelia.

Kuttner snatched it up, handed it over.

"Just find her, Mr. Healy."

28.

Holly was asleep now. It seemed like all of L.A. was, except for Holland March and Jackson Healy. March was sitting on the diving board of the swimming pool behind his house, a bottle of whiskey beside him, staring down into the concrete depths of the pool, which he'd never bothered to fill. Not with water, anyway. There was a nice layer of cigarette butts down there, and it was growing. Los Angeles, home of the world's biggest ashtray.

Fuck it, it was a rental. They were only here until they could rebuild the old place. He'd tried explaining this to Healy when the guy started riding his ass for all the butts in the pool. "My house burned down," he said. "Just like that place we drove to. *Whoof.* Like Chet said. It actually sounded like that when it happened. *Whoof.*"

"Sorry."

"Yeah." March took another pull of the whiskey. Wiped the neck of the bottle, held it out to Healy, but the bastard turned it down again.

"What the hell? Do I have bad breath or something?"

"Nah," Healy said, "I just have this allergy to alcohol."

"Really?"

"Yeah, I break out in handcuffs."

"Funny," March said, but he put the bottle back down, didn't push it. It's not like he'd never felt the impulse to quit himself. He'd never given in to it, but it's not like he'd never had the impulse.

"Hey," Healy said, "you know, something's actually bugging me. Kuttner's prosecuting this car case, right? And the two guys who were coming after Amelia, they were from around Detroit. The guy up at the hot tub told me he'd go back to Michigan. And the dead guy? I took a look in his wallet before Holly came back. His name was Gilbert Dufresne, from Livonia, Michigan."

"So?"

"So the car companies would certainly have a reason to want to see Kuttner brought down. They'd love to get their hands on that film, use it to blackmail her."

"Okay."

"But what I don't get is why they'd want Amelia dead. You'd think they'd love her, if she was out to embarrass her mother. Enemy of my enemy, right?"

"Sure," March said. He hadn't been listening.

"Plus," Healy said, "I found this in Shattuck's office." He took the cow-shaped slip of paper out of his pocket. It was crumpled and water-stained from his adventure at the hot tub, but it was still readable:

28-10 Burbank Apt
West, Flt D, 10:30pm

March leaned forward precariously to peer at it. "What is that, a pig?"

"No," Healy said, "it's a pink cow."

"Oh, a cow."

"When Amelia gave me your address," Healy said,

"she gave it to me on a piece of paper like this, hand-writing like that. So I'm thinking Amelia wrote that too, and that might mean she was planning to fly somewhere. Flight D, Burbank Airport."

March sat back up again, somewhat unsteadily. "I think you're on to something. Can we talk about it tomorrow? …afternoon?"

Healy threw up his hands. This guy. "Yeah. We can do that."

"Thanks."

March took another long drink, and Healy started walking away, back toward the house.

"Hey…" March said, with a grin. "Aren't you that diner guy…?"

Healy gave him his meanest look, up from under lowered brows. Normally it might've scared March, but he was drunk as fuck and nothing on God's green earth would've scared him right now. Besides, Healy didn't look that scary once you got to know him. He practically looked cuddly, for chrissakes. That curl of hair hanging down over his forehead like a little boy, that hangdog expression when he didn't want to talk about something.

"Come on," Healy begged him, "come on come on come on come on come on. I gotta know."

"I don't want to get into it."

"You've *gotta* get into it. You're the diner guy." He smiled, shrugged. Like it was the law and he was just following orders. He remembered the moves from his days on the beat.

Healy sighed a deep sigh, one that seemed to come

from somewhere around the middle of his chest. "All right."

"Yes!" March got himself comfortable on his diving-board perch, lay back with his legs hanging off the end, let his eyes drift shut and just listened to Healy's voice. The man had one hell of a voice. Rough and low but somehow reassuring. He could have had a side job narrating nature documentaries.

"All right," Healy began. "About a year ago, I was at a diner in Hollywood. A Denny's."

"Yes."

"This asshole with a shotgun started threatening people," Healy went on.

"I love it," Healy mumbled. "It's the best story I've ever heard."

"So I did something about it," Healy said. "I acted. I didn't plan to, I didn't, you know… I just did it."

Healy was standing comfortably on the deck of an empty swimming pool, a cool breeze teasing his cheeks and ruffling his hair, but he was also remembering what it had felt like to be seated at that counter, to hear the blast and the shells ringing as they were ejected onto the floor. The people screaming. Dishes breaking.

The smell of gunpowder in the air.

"I took that guy out," he said. "I didn't even get paid for it. I ended up with a bullet in the bicep and five hundred dollars of hospital bills. It was stupid, really."

It was a smell that stayed with you, gunpowder. He was smelling it for days, even after he got back from the hospital. His fish had been so fucking hungry when they finally saw him again, they ate half a can of fish food in one meal. He'd fed it to them with fingers that stank of sulfur and gunsmoke.

His fish. His poor goddamn fish.

"When I think about it," Healy said, and he paused a little to think about it now, "it was the best day of my life."

He looked over at the diving board. March was sprawled out on it, softly snoring.

"Just for a moment," Healy said quietly, "I felt useful."

He left March where he was. Yeah, maybe the little prick would roll over in the night and break his neck, but somehow he'd gotten through life so far with nothing worse than a broken arm to show for it, so Healy was prepared to believe March would make it through one more night. Some guys just had a guardian angel watching over them. Whether they deserved it or not.

He headed inside. On his way to the front door, he noticed that Holly's bedroom door was open. The bedclothes were shoved back, the bed empty.

Driving back toward home, Healy saw a small figure sitting Indian-fashion on the ground of the vacant lot down the block. She had a flashlight in her lap, pointed at the pages of a book.

He stopped the car, got out.

"'Had Mademoiselle Blanche been in England before? What part of France did she come from? Mademoiselle Blanche replied politely but with reserve—'" Holly looked up. Healy's shadow had fallen over the page.

"Hey," he said.

"Hey." She stared at him. "You've got your foot in the toilet," she said.

"I have?" He lifted his leg, shook the imaginary water off his cuff.

Holly sighed. "Now you're getting the carpet all wet."

"Was this your room?" Healy asked.

"No," she said. "It was mom and dad's."

Healy looked off toward the horizon, which wasn't visible yet. The dawn was some way off. "Your dad tells me you're rebuilding."

"Does it look rebuilt to you?"

"Not especially."

"Dad barely ever comes here," she said. "Feels guilty, I guess."

"Because…?"

She looked up. "Hm? Oh. The fire." She shook her head ruefully but her voice stayed matter-of-fact. "Mom kept complaining about a leak in the furnace, but dad, you know, he's got his nose thing, so…he couldn't smell the gas."

Healy looked off. He didn't have anything much to say to that.

"Anyways," Holly said. "I…I should probably get back to my book."

"All right." Healy started off toward his car.

Holly called out to him before he'd gotten too far. "Mr. Healy…?"

Healy stopped, turned back.

"Are you a bad person?"

Healy didn't say anything, just stood there in the dark.

"What did you do to that man tonight? Did you kill him?"

It was so comfortable to stand in the dark, to talk without anyone being able to see your face or look you in the eye. "Of course not," Healy said.

"That's good," Holly said. "I knew you couldn't do something like that."

Healy thought of a million things he might say to her. *Grow up, kid* or *Don't you understand, he was dying anyway* or *That man needed to be gone, the world was a better place the instant he stopped breathing*—any of that, or, if you wanted to go the other way, maybe something like *No of course not, honey, I'm not a killer, I hurt people sometimes, like I hurt your dad, but I don't kill them, honest injun. Scout's honor.*

But he didn't say any of these things. "Don't stay up too late, all right?"

He saw her nod, her chin dipping into and out of the flashlight beam.

Good enough.

He picked his way back to his car.

29.

The next day found Healy sitting on the front stoop at March's place, a couple of takeout containers in a plastic bag beside him. Even though it was afternoon, like they'd agreed, he'd picked up breakfast stuff from an all-day diner, figuring March would've slept late, and maybe Holly, too—she'd had a tough night of her own. But when he'd knocked, he'd found no one home. So he'd sat and waited. The pancakes and eggs had gone cold, but then the orange juice had gotten warm, so how's that inertia for you?

March's car eventually pulled in, the front tires bumping up over the curb. Healy watched Holly shut off the ignition and clamber out of the driver's seat, quietly fuming. Her dad, in the passenger seat, had been keeping time to the music blasting out of the radio with one hand, pounding out the beat on the door frame, and he stopped only reluctantly when the sound cut off. He saw Healy sitting there and muttered, "Shit," remembering. He got out, a suit bag slung over one shoulder, cigarette between his lips, big, fake smile plastered on his face. Healy got the sense it wasn't the only thing that had gotten plastered this afternoon.

He stood, held up the takeout. "Didn't know what time you'd get here. Some of it's probably still good."

"Sorry," March said, stifling a belch with his fist, "we

were at the bank. Getting your money." He pulled an envelope out of his pocket. "There it is. Half. Minus a few hundred, you know, for the…that car that we crashed? I thought you'd want to chip in for that."

He was wincing a little, like maybe he thought Healy might explode over that "we," but Healy just shrugged it off. "Sure."

March handed over the envelope on the way to the door, Holly a few steps ahead of him. He held up the suit bag, unzipped it far enough to show off a lapel. "What do you think?" It looked bright even through Healy's shades.

"It's purple," Healy said.

"It's maroon," March said. He zipped it up again. "Saw it in the window of this store, had to try it on. Sorry we were late."

"It's okay."

But Holly had had enough. "The store took ten minutes. We stopped at a bar. That's why we're late."

She pushed past Healy and stormed into the house.

Healy followed, set his Styrofoam containers on the counter. March came last, shutting the door behind him. The tension was so thick you could've cut it with a knife, though probably not one of the plastic ones they'd given him with the pancakes.

"So," he said, "want to talk about the case?" He took the by now well-worn cow-shaped slip of paper from his pocket, held it up.

28-10 Burbank Apt
West, Flt D, 10:30pm

"Burbank Airport?" he said. "Western Airlines? I'm thinking she's trying to skip town. How do you want to do this?"

"Well," March said, on his way from the kitchen to the living room with a glass in one fist, ice cubes tinkling in a whiskey bath, "I say we wait a couple of days, call Kuttner, and see if we can squeeze a second installment out of her."

Healy was nonplussed. "Second installment…?"

It was Holly who answered. She knew the drill. "You don't want to call too soon. Got to act like you're on to something, like you've been working hard…then, day three, ask for more money." She plopped down on one of the stools by the kitchen counter and crossed her arms over her chest.

Healy looked from daughter to father.

"Well, she's putting a negative spin on it," March said, "but yeah, that's the idea."

"Kuttner *paid* us," Healy said. "She paid *me*, to do a job. All right? I'm not going to lie to her."

"And I respect that," March said, taking a swallow. "So I'll lie to her."

"Hey," Healy said, angry now, "forget Kuttner, *I* shelled out four hundred bucks for a detective, someone who finds clues—"

"I found Sid Shattuck's corpse, didn't I?"

"Found it? You fell on it! You fall down a manhole, you don't say, look, I found the sewer."

March shrugged. Tomato, to-mah-to. "I guess I don't understand why we're not celebrating," he said, heading back to the refrigerator. Needed more ice. "I mean, we just got paid, we're all having a drink in the afternoon…" He looked at Healy, at Holly, and they stared back. "What?"

Healy just said, "Forget about it." He headed for the door.

"Aw, would you just, would you hold on for a goddamn second?" He tossed back the rest of his whiskey, swung the freezer open for more ice. Pinned to the freezer door with a magnet was his ad from the Yellow Pages, a line drawing of his face looking young, handsome, and not at all drunk, next to the words *LICENSED AND BONDED*. "THE HOLLAND MARCH AGENCY," the ad said. "Our trained investigators have specialized in CLOSING CASES since 1972."

Holly shook her head, a look of profound disappointment on her face. "You're the world's worst detective," she said.

March didn't know what to say to that. "I'm the worst?"

"Yes."

"The *world's* worst?"

"Didn't you hear me the first time?"

"Got a cool ad, though." He dropped ice into his drink, plunk, plunk, plunk. "So."

But Holly wasn't letting him weasel out with a joke this time. "Why do you have to be such a fuck-up? Huh? You go around and…and you drink, and you lie and stuff, and people hate you!"

"Sweetheart, don't say 'and stuff,' just say—"

"*I hate you!*"

"That works," March said.

Healy headed for the door again. "I'll find the girl myself."

"You're going to find her yourself," March muttered. "Okay." He called out to Healy's departing back, "Well, say hi to her when you do."

"I will."

" 'Course you're not going to find her at the airport," he said, "seeing as how it's not a flight."

Healy was out of March's line of sight already, and March turned to Holly. "Did he stop?"

She nodded sullenly.

"Your note," March called out. "Look at it. It's not a flight."

Healy looked at it. *28-10 Burbank Apt West, Flt D, 10:30pm.*

March got to his feet. He wasn't staggering now, he wasn't slurring. He was quoting the note from memory, was what he was doing. "*Twenty-eight ten, Burbank A-P-T, ten-thirty.* Well, every airport has an overflight curfew from ten to six, Burbank included. So no ten-thirty flights. And that top number? It's today's date, but reversed, like the European way, *twenty-eight ten* instead of *ten twenty-eight.* Which makes sense when you look at 'F-L-T' and you think, that's not flight, it's probably *flat*, like apartment."

Healy just stood there, thunderstruck. Where the hell had all that come from?

Holly looked pretty damn shocked as well. Who'd replaced her father with an actual detective?

"And Burbank A-P-T?" Healy said.

"West," March said. "Burbank A-P-T *West*—the Burbank Apartments West, it's a dump, down by the— Fuck it, I'll show you." He set his glass down on the edge of the sink, walked past Healy to where his daughter was sitting. "If Amelia's going to be there at ten-thirty, we'll want to get there twenty minutes earlier so we can stake out the lobby. If I remember correctly, there's both front and rear entrances at the old Burbank West, so it's good there's two of us. I'll take the front, since there's at least a chance she doesn't know what I look like, and you—you can stay in the car, and keep your head down, for Christ's sake." Finally, to Holly: "You're going to Janet's, but for real, this time."

"Jessica's," Holly said.

"Jessica's."

Normally she'd have argued. But right now she just nodded. Was that a hint of a smile on her face? Was that pride in her eyes?

Fuck-up, huh? March looked over to where Healy was standing, looking equally impressed. Who's the fuck-up now?

30.

Healy stepped on the brakes and the car slewed to a stop across the street from a vacant lot only slightly more developed than the one March's daughter liked to read in. There was a bulldozer in one corner and some stacks of lumber in another. Some grass on the ground.

No apartments, west, east, or otherwise.

Healy looked over at March in the passenger seat.

An old geezer was passing the site, walking a hairy poodle on a leash. "Excuse me," Healy called out, and the guy stopped. "We're looking for the Burbank Apartments."

"Oh, they're gone," the guy said. "Tore them babies down going on about two years now." He kept on walking, dragging the dog behind.

Healy turned to March.

March didn't blink. He pointed in the direction of northern Burbank. "To the airport, then?"

31

Healy was driving as fast as his car would go. They'd been twenty minutes early to the vacant lot, but it would take a miracle for them to get to the airport less than ten minutes late.

"Well, they *used* to have an overflight curfew," March was saying.

"All right," Healy said. "It's all right. It's okay."

"They did."

"Yeah."

"And they still should. If they changed, then they should. They should change it back."

Traffic was light, thankfully. Healy wished March's chatter was too. But it wasn't. He tried to block it out, and was halfway successful. Every few seconds, some sentence or phrase would break through and land annoyingly in his ears, making him grip the steering wheel tighter and grind his teeth.

He was trying to put his finger on just what it was he found so annoying about Holland March. It wasn't that he was a bad detective—who was Healy to complain about that? He was hardly Sherlock fucking Holmes himself. And it wasn't the man's lack of ethics. Well, partly. But it's not like Healy was Benedict fucking Spinoza. (And yes, he'd read Spinoza, thank you very much. Part of the curriculum down on the farm, they'd fed them

Spinoza and Augustine and Thomas Aquinas along with all those goddamned avocados, and though he'd sooner cut his own balls off with a fingernail clipper than slog through Aquinas again, he'd always kind of thought of Spinoza as something of a kindred spirit deep down. Put a set of brass knucks in that guy's hands, he'd have known how to take care of business.)

So, no, it wasn't any of that, and it wasn't even the motor-mouthed gibbering that just never fucking stopped, unless the guy drank himself into a stupor. Though right at this moment, a stupor might have been welcome. No, what it was was, the man didn't have any idea how good he had it. Yeah, sure, he'd lost his wife and his house in a terrible accident, okay. Healy gave him that. But man, he had this great daughter, he had a job where he could set his own rules and answer to nobody and maybe do some good in the world, he was young and healthy, if you didn't look too close at what had to be a liver on the edge of collapse, and he lived within spitting distance of the Pacific Ocean, where on a good day you could dip your toes in the same water that washes up on the beaches of Hawaii. He wasn't a fucking accountant in Boise, or a salesman wearing out his tires up and down the northeast, never seeing another soul who was glad to see him coming. He wasn't that poor bastard whose job it was to mop Gilbert Dufresne's blood up off the highway at midnight. And, not to put too fine a point on it, he wasn't a knee-breaker living in one room over a comedy club, either, though it was a very nice room and Healy was glad to have it. No, March was sitting pretty, or could've been, but instead he seemed always on the verge of chewing his leg off to escape some trap, like running his mouth was the only thing keeping him from breaking into a run the old-fashioned way. What it came down to was, the man constantly seemed scared. And why? What was he so scared of? Having to face himself in the goddamn mirror?

Healy took that moment to face himself in the goddamn mirror, take a good look at a what a middle-aged ex-avocado farmer looked like. Not too bad. Maybe not handsome like playboy over there, a few too many bruises and scars, but—

"Pull over," March said suddenly.

Healy was drawn out of his reverie. "What?"

"Pull over, pull over." March was aiming a thumb out the window, looking up at a glass-and-steel tower with fancy elevators climbing the sides. "She's not going to the airport."

Healy bent to look up through the windshield at the giant letters March was pointing out.

The sign for the Burbank Airport Western Hotel cast a bright glow over the pavement. Behind it, maybe half a mile away, a jetliner climbed, climbed, and was gone. "She's not flying. She's meeting somebody."

Come in for a landing, a smaller sign on the hotel's wall said. *Visit THE FLIGHT DECK Lounge.*

Flt D.

"Okay," Healy said. "Let's go."

32.

Sometime around midnight, no doubt, the Flight Deck Lounge would be a happening spot, where businessmen visiting L.A. for a convention would put the moves on their female assistants or find a lady of the evening to rock them to sleep instead. But that was more than an hour away, and for now the room was empty, the only sound in the place coming from the bartender, a rat-faced character with a hand-painted necktie and wiry goatee who was racking glasses in anticipation of the coming rush.

Healy and March bellied up to the bar.

"Evening," the barkeep said, wiping his hands on a towel. "What can I get you?"

"Information," March said. He held up the photo of Amelia they'd gotten from Kuttner. "You seen this girl? She probably came in in the last half hour…?"

"Hey, I just work here," the guy said.

"No shit, Sherlock, that's why I'm asking you," March said.

"Yeah, well. Memory gets a little foggy, you know." The guy leaned forward from his side of the bar, tie dangling down into his little tub of olives. "What's in it for me?"

"He'll stop doing it," March said, pointing at Healy beside him.

"Doing what?"

Healy snatched the man's tie in his fist, used it to pull his forehead down in a swift, sharp smack against the wood of the bar.

"Ow!"

"That," March said.

The man was holding his head. "Fuck!"

"Now, we can do this the easy way," Healy said, "or we can—" He paused. Maybe some clarification was in order. "We're currently doing it the easy way," he said.

"Okay! Jesus," the barkeep said. "The penthouse. She's in the penthouse, top floor." He rubbed the bruised spot over his eyebrow. "Are you happy?"

"Yeah," March said, and they turned to leave.

"Guys, listen," the barkeep said. "You don't want to go up there. Trust me."

March and Healy came back.

"These New York guys are up there," the barkeep said, his voice anxious. "Business guys. They got these fucking bodyguards, the kind that had their balls removed, you know what I mean? What's that called again?"

"Marriage," Healy muttered.

"Just chill here," the barkeep urged them. "She's gonna come back down. Have a couple cold ones on me…"

"Oh, not for me," Healy said.

"He makes a strong argument, though," March said. Anyone offering free booze was making a strong argument as far as March was concerned.

"You see?" the barkeep said, moving to fill a couple of glasses. "Reasonable. Very reasonable. Now, your buddy? That was a problem, he wasn't reasonable."

Healy lowered his gaze. "Our buddy?"

"The other guy looking for Amelia," the barkeep said. He put the glasses down in front of them. "He wasn't with you?"

March shot Healy a look. "We don't have friends," he told the barkeep.

"Where'd he go?" Healy asked. "This friend."

"Got in the elevator," the barkeep said, "right before you fellows came in."

"Did you get a name?" Healy asked, trying to keep his voice casual.

"John something."

Fuck. "Did you actually witness him getting into the elevator?"

The guy's voice dripped with sarcasm when he answered. "No, it was told to me by a wise old Indian. Of course I fucking witnessed it."

"Right," Healy said. "Thanks."

March drank his beer, waited till the bartender had wandered over to the other end of the bar, then bent in close, so the guy couldn't overhear. "What the hell's going on?"

"Oh, it just makes sense," Healy said, in a mild, calm voice. "Connects up." There was no sense in panicking March. If he acted scared under the best of circumstances—

"What makes sense?" March asked.

"John-Boy," Healy said. "Just something that Dufresne mentioned."

"What do you mean, he mentioned? Mentioned how?"

"Oh, you know," Healy said, "just, 'There's a guy, comin' to kill you,' that kind of crap." He rolled his eyes.

It did exactly zero good. March panicked. Healy could tell because his cheek kept twitching, even after he'd reached over and drunk Healy's beer.

"We should probably just stay here," March said.

"Smart move," Healy admitted. "Unless, of course, he's up there killing her right now."

"Come on, nobody's getting killed at the Burbank Airport Hotel."

"Because…?"

"That would be national news," March said.

"Yeah? So?"

"Oh? So when's the last time you were on the national news?"

"February," Healy said.

"Really?"

"Yeah."

March was incredulous. "For what?"

"I got shot," Healy said. "In the diner."

"You got shot? Where?"

"In my arm." Healy pointed to his bicep. "I told you this last night."

"I don't remember you telling me," March said.

"Guess you were asleep."

March nodded, and they both took a moment to consider the situation. Healy didn't especially want to get shot again, and March clearly didn't want to get shot for the first time. But sometimes you had to do what you had to do.

"We should call the cops," March said.

"No, that'll take too long," Healy said. "I mean, she could die."

"You just said it was the right move to stay down here," March said.

"No, I said smart move. Different."

They stared at each other. Neither of them much wanted to go.

But no one had ever accused them of being smart.

They headed for the elevator.

The Muzak playing over the concealed speaker should've helped calm their jangled nerves, but if anything it made March more tense. He found himself fidgeting, feeling the weight of the cast on his arm, wishing he hadn't had that second drink downstairs. Not that two beers was too many. Just, you know, two in two minutes. The indicator ticked off the floors as they rose. Penthouse, huh? At least it gave them some time to get mentally prepared to face this guy who was supposedly there to kill them.

They called him John-Boy, like the kid on *The Waltons*? What did that mean? That he had a mole and a bad hair-cut? That he'd been around during the Depression? That would be nice, since it would mean he'd be in his sixties now, maybe not so spry anymore. Or did it just mean his name was John? Maybe his last name was Boy. You never knew. March had a cousin named April, April March. She'd hated her parents.

He blinked a bunch.

"Munich," he said, and Healy turned to look at him.

"What?"

The word had just come to him, out of nowhere. "Guy without his balls. A munich."

"Munich," Healy said, "is a city in Germany. *München*. Munich. Yeah."

"You sure?"

"My dad was stationed there."

"Right." March thought for a moment longer. "Hitler only had one ball," he said.

Before Healy could respond to that nugget of wisdom, the elevator bell pinged and the doors started to open. "All right," he muttered, grateful for the reprieve. "Here we go."

Before he could step out, though—before either of them could—they heard a sound from the corridor outside, something in between a cough and a wheeze. Looking out, they saw a man staggering toward them with one hand clutched to his throat. He was bald, bearded. No way of knowing what knife work he'd had done on him below the belt, but what he'd gotten above the necktie was pretty clear. Blood spilled out over his hand from a gaping slash, and he collapsed, face down on the wall-to-wall carpet.

From the opposite direction came the sound of punches landing—one, two, like a slugger working out with a heavy bag in the gym. Then a man in a white tux fell back a few steps, caught between a bend in the corridor and the floor-to-ceiling glass picture window beside the elevator.

Bullets followed him—from a gun with a silencer, judging by the sound—and blood bloomed on the man's white jacket like so many red carnations. The glass behind him starred as the bullets struck it.

Healy and March pulled their heads back into the elevator.

March jabbed the Close Door button.

After a second, the doors slowly slid shut.

Healy didn't say anything, and neither did March. They just faced forward. Listened to the Muzak. Until the sound of shattering glass and a man's scream interrupted the soothing melody. They both turned to look and saw the man in the white tux go tumbling through the broken window, falling past them, out of sight.

They faced forward again, waited patiently for the elevator to reach the lobby.

March's blinking was worse.

When the bell pinged at the bottom, they strode out, crossing the lobby in fewer steps than either of them would've thought possible. They found the car right where they'd left it and sank into its bucket seats gratefully. Healy stepped on the gas and they roared off.

But not fast enough—just half a block away they heard police sirens coming from the other direction. To avoid them, Healy took a sharp turn into a service alley behind the hotel. The cop cars zoomed past, four or five of them. Someone must've called it in, maybe the rat-faced bartender. All the more reason to get away while they could.

March waited for Healy to slam into reverse and back out of the alley, but Healy didn't.

"What are we doing?" March asked.

"I can't just leave," Healy said.

"Why?"

"She's in danger, man. We have to do something about it."

"Are you nuts? It's over. We stay, we could go down for it."

"Why?" Healy said. "We didn't do anything."

"Think," March said. "We shoved that bartender around, we asked him about Amelia, we went upstairs—"

"Even so," Healy said. "We've still got to help her."

"She's *dead*," March said, and something in his voice made it clear he expected the two of them to join her at any minute.

"What do you mean, she's dead?"

"Come on!"

"She's not dead," Healy insisted.

"Open your eyes, man! She's fucking dead!"

"You don't know that."

The calmer Healy sounded, the more hysterical March got. He was screaming now, in a high-pitched voice that would've done his daughter credit.

Suddenly a loud bang silenced them both and the car shook as if something heavy had just landed on the roof. A second later, two bare feet came into view through the windshield, climbing down onto the hood of the car. Then the hem of a canary-yellow dress.

"Amelia," March whispered.

"I told you she wasn't dead."

Standing unsteadily on the hood, Amelia Kuttner bent to look in at them through the windshield. March gave her a pained smile, and she started in recognition. She swung her arm up, revealing a handgun gripped tightly in her fist, and fired right at them.

Fortunately, after smashing a golf ball-sized hole in the glass, the bullet sailed harmlessly between them, lodging in the back seat cushion. Amelia, meanwhile, was propelled backward off the hood by the recoil, landing in the alley in front of the car. They heard a loud clunk, and when they both leaped out and ran to her side, they found that she'd knocked herself unconscious against the pavement.

March looked up at the dangling fire escape from which she'd jumped down onto the car and back at the unconscious girl.

More sirens sounded in the distance.

"Help me with her," Healy said.

They were old hands at this now. They resumed their Sid Shattuck positions—Healy at head, March at feet—and bundled her into the car.

They left the gun behind.

33.

On the black-and-white television screen, a little glowing ball was bouncing back and forth between two paddles. Well, two vertical lines, anyway. Holly wasn't too impressed. She knew every kid in L.A. was dying to play these things—Studio II, Atari, Telstar, whatever—but she didn't know why her dad, who after all was a grown-up, had bought one.

Between electronic boops, she heard a key in the front door lock. She jumped up as her father came in, his nice blue suit all rumpled.

March was as startled to see her as she was to see him. "What are you doing here?" he said.

"Holy shit!" she shouted. Healy had just come through the door with the unconscious Amelia draped across his arms. "You got her!"

"You're supposed to be at Jessica's," March said.

Jessica stood up from the couch, video-game controller in one hand, looking apologetic. "Yeah, sorry, Mr. March, my sister kicked us out, she's having a guy over."

"Your sister's such a slut," March said.

"Yeah, I know." She put the controller down, and they all followed Healy into Holly's bedroom, where he dumped Amelia unceremoniously on Holly's bed. It didn't wake her up, though she moaned slightly.

"Hello?" Healy said, gently. "Amelia?"

"Should we shake her shoulder?" March asked.

"You know, my brother used to flick my ear, like that." Healy demonstrated. "I hated that."

Holly said, "We shouldn't be violent," and at almost the exact same moment Jessica said, "We could just hit her." The best friends looked at each other in mutual disbelief.

"It could really hurt, I guess," Jessica said, backing down. "I guess it's not practical."

"We probably shouldn't hit her if we want her to talk to us," Healy said.

They all agreed that was sensible. Anyway, it looked like maybe Amelia was stirring now. She was on her side, one arm stretched out above her head, and yes, her eyelids were definitely fluttering.

In fact, Amelia was awake, having come to just in time to hear the suggestion that she be hit. She didn't know where she was or who was standing around her, though a couple of the voices sounded reassuringly like little girls. Still. It was sometimes wise to wait a little, get your head together, before letting the people around you know you were on to them.

She'd learned this the hard way in the movement, which is to say the protest group she'd founded and very nearly gotten kicked out of during a factional dispute last summer. Not a very different situation than this one, actually, though it hadn't involved quite so much literal bloodshed. There'd been a party, and a lot of her friends had been there, they'd argued long into the night about tactics and strategy, the way you do when half the room is on pot and the other half is on acid; and then they'd fallen asleep, but she'd awakened to the sound of her first lieutenant, a chick named Maureen, explaining to everyone else in the Steering Committee why she, Amelia, was a traitor to their cause and needed to be voted out of the group immediately.

It hadn't been easy keeping her eyes closed then, but she'd done it, and listened to the entire conversation, filing away in her head just who it was that came to her defense and who fell in line for Maureen's little putsch. Naturally, it was the boys who thought Maureen was a genius. She'd listened and she'd heard, and then, when the discussion had moved on to other things—pollution, music, how nice Maureen's tits were—she'd calmly stretched and "woken up," and no one in the room knew she'd been awake for the whole thing. She had set things right over the following week, cleaning house, real Michael Corleone-type shit, leaving just her loyal crew in the group, and ever since that she'd had no problems. I mean, there were problems, of course, you always had problems in a protest group—not enough gas masks, whatever. But no betrayals from within. And all because she'd kept her eyes closed and listened.

Which is what she was doing now. But they'd stopped talking, and clearly were just waiting for her to do or say something, so fuck it. She was awake.

She let her eyelids flutter open.

This was definitely a young girl's room. And yeah, there were two of them standing there at the foot of the bed, staring at her like she was stuffed and mounted in a museum diorama. Then to either side of the bed—

That guy! One of the ones she'd hired Healy to get off her back! He had a cast on his arm, so that was something, but clearly it hadn't been enough. And on the other side, Healy himself, looking down at her with dad-like concern.

"You were supposed to get those guys off of me," she said to him. *Dad.*

"It's okay," Healy said. "You're safe."

"Do you know who they were? Who sent them?" This from the guy in the cast with the droopy I'm-hip-too 'stache, the one who by all accounts had been chasing after her for the past week, asking about her in every joint from Pegleg's to the Iron Horse. March.

"Yeah," Amelia said, turning over and burying her face in the pillow again, "my mother."

Healy bent down, hands on his knees, face close to hers. "Would you mind starting from the top…?"

She rolled over again, the other way. "Why? Doesn't matter!" She hated how whiny her voice sounded. But it *didn't* matter, that was the truth. These two clowns couldn't protect her, whether they knew the whole story or not. Her mother would grind them up and make sausages out of them. That's what guys like this were: sausage meat. Why'd she ever thought she could rely on Healy to be anything more?

"I'm sorry, 'doesn't matter'? You just shot at us, I think it matters." March was pissed. Boo-hoo.

But, eh, it was clear they weren't going to leave her alone till she told them something. And right now, with her head hurting and her knee hurting and, god, *everything* hurting, it was easier to just tell them the truth than to make something up.

"Okay, okay," she said. "I made a film. I made a film with Dean, my boyfriend." She sat up halfway, pulled her dress down when she caught March staring, the fucking pervert. "The idea was that we were going to, you know, like, make this experimental film? Like, an artistic film."

"Porno film?" March said, and she sat up the rest of the way.

"It's not a porno!" God! She wanted to scream. But she held it in. "Do you even know who my mother is?" she asked.

"Yes," Healy said. "We do. We've, we've actually met your mother, and—"

"What'd she tell you? That I'm crazy? That I'm just 'lashing out'…?"

"Something like that," Healy acknowledged. "She might have mentioned—"

Amelia flopped back down on the pillows. "Yeah, well? My mother is a criminal. She's one of Them."

"Who's 'Them'?" March asked. "What's 'Them'?"

"One of the insiders," Amelia said, her voice shaking with frustration. Why was it so hard for people to see the truth and understand it? They didn't want to. That's what it boiled down to, they led comfortable bourgeois lives and they just didn't want to. "One of the capitalist… corporate…suppressors! You know they want us dead, man. We're just in their crosshairs, you know. We're just pawns!"

"Gosh," said one of the little girls at the foot of the

bed, the brown-haired one. She looked like maybe she was ready to be enlightened. The blonde was looking at her more cynically, with her arms crossed, like a little William F. Buckley, Jr.

Amelia threw herself back petulantly, expecting a pillow behind her, but her head clonked painfully against the wall. "Ow," she said.

"Hey," March said, and he whistled, like the pig he was, and the girls marched out of the bedroom. Like the pawns they were.

March resumed questioning her, with less patience in his voice this time. "What does this have to do with the birds?"

And Healy chimed in: "Yeah."

"My mom's supposed to be working for the Justice Department, right?"

"Sure," Healy said, "she's prosecuting the catalytic converter case."

"Yeah, only she's not. She's not prosecuting it. The automakers, she's gonna let them walk."

"But they have the evidence," March said.

"*Yes* they have evidence!" Amelia shouted. "They have memos proving that Detroit conspired to suppress the converter, proving they would rather poison our air than spend a little bit of money. But my mom, she's going to say that's not enough, she's going to lie, because she's on the take. Right? Money again, Mammon, that's her god, that, that…fascist…crony…Bogart…"

"Okay, okay," Healy said, patting the air, "just…just back up a little bit."

She lay down again. Carefully. Her head couldn't take another whack.

Healy looked like he was struggling for words. "Why not just go straight to the police?" he asked finally.

Amelia couldn't help laughing. These guys were so blind. "She *is* the police! She's the head of the Justice Department!"

She saw March's eyes open wider at that.

"You got a point," Healy said.

"Okay," March said, "or the newspapers…?"

"They all work together," Amelia said. "God! You been living under a rock?"

"Okay," Healy said. "So then your solution was…you make a porn film?"

"It's not a porno!" Top of her lungs, to get the message across once and for all.

"You know, I have neighbors," March said.

"I made a *statement*," Amelia said. "And yeah, yeah, my statement contained nudity—art—"

"Porno nudity," March said.

"That's just the commercial element, okay?" she spat back. "Okay? Sid said we had to have that. And the reality was, we were getting our message out there. And, and, it was all in the film: names, and dates, and everything— everything! Everything my mom was doing. And once it was out there, once it was in theaters, there was no way that they could suppress it. There was no way that they could cover it up."

"So let me get this straight," March said. "You made a porno film where the point was the *plot*?"

She sighed. She just wasn't getting through. "What's your hangup, man?"

"So, it's not the sex," Healy said, "it's what's in the story. That's why the film's so important to them. They don't want to use it to embarrass your mom, they want it out of circulation to keep it from embarrassing them. Or worse."

All right. At least one of them was getting it.

"My mom found out," Amelia said. "She killed Dean and destroyed the film."

"Your mom killed Dean?" Healy didn't sound like he quite believed this. Maybe he wasn't getting it after all. The older generation could be so dense! Even when they wanted to help. Their brains were like, fixed. Set. Like concrete.

"Of course," Amelia said. "She killed Misty, too."

"And Sid Shattuck…?" This came from the blonde girl, who was standing in the doorway, her brown-haired friend behind her looking on curiously. The blonde's arms were still crossed, but she sounded less skeptical than her, her *parents* here.

"Yeah," Amelia said. "Sid, too."

"Okay, so it's like Jack the Ripper, and then your mom," March said. "Basically."

The blonde girl had come back into the room. "So what are you going to do?"

"I don't know." Amelia rolled over, plumped up the pillow under her head. "I'm just really tired, you know?" And she was. God. So tired.

"All right, okay," Healy said, standing up, "So, you… we're just gonna talk about it, think on it, and you get some rest." He covered her up a bit with her dress, which had slid off her thigh. Such a dad.

"Yeah," March said, "just get some rest."

34.

They looked in through the open doorway. Amelia seemed to be sleeping again.

"What do you think?" Healy asked, keeping his voice low.

"I like her," Holly said.

"I like her dress," Jessica said.

"It's a nice dress," March agreed. Then he turned to Healy. "But she's a loon. According to her, her mother is single-handedly going to wipe out all of Western society." There was that expression again, single-handedly. You couldn't get away from it.

"Yeah, however," Healy said, "there *are* people trying to kill her, right? Like John-Boy."

"Who's John-Boy?" Holly wanted to know.

"He's on *The Waltons*," Jessica informed her. It was one of the only shows Jessica's parents let her watch, probably out of fear that she might turn out like her sister otherwise.

"No," Healy said, "different John-Boy."

"Well, we think," said March.

"We think, yeah. Pretty sure."

"You can't be sure, though," March said. The phone rang, and he ran to get it. Wouldn't want to wake up the sleeping loony bird. Let her get her loony-bird rest.

He grabbed the phone on the second ring.

"Mr. March?" The voice was halfway familiar. Then it was all the way familiar, and March smiled—it was Tally. The night was looking up. But…why would she be calling? "I just got a call from Judith. She didn't explain herself, just said she needed one hundred thousand dollars in cash."

"A hundred thousand dollars? Why?"

"I don't know," Tally said. "I think she's involved in something…shady, maybe?"

"Well, her daughter certainly seems to think so."

"What, Amelia? You found Amelia?"

"Yes! She fell on our car! We were just talking, and she fell on our car. Anyway, she's here, you should come over…"

"She okay? I'll, I'll send the family doctor," Tally said. She sounded so pleased, so relieved. But there was still an edge to her voice. "Mr. March—"

"Holland, please."

"—I've got a bad feeling about this. Judith's call, I mean. I don't know what's going on. Would you…would you be willing to carry the money for me?"

"I wish I knew who to believe on this one," Healy was saying, and March thought the answer to that was pretty obvious. You believed the beautiful lady who was about to trust you with one hundred thousand dollars. They were walking along the concrete stretch from the street to Kuttner's office building, having left March's convertible by the curb.

"Well, the kid's a write-off, I'll tell you that much,"

March opined. He lifted a telephone handset hanging beside the front door and pressed the intercom button. "We're downstairs."

"Maybe they're both telling the truth," Healy said.

March hung up the phone. "She's coming down." He turned to Healy, whose last cryptic comment had just sunk in. "What you do mean, they're both telling the truth? What does that mean?"

Healy thought a bit. "I got a friend, right? Secret Service. Worked the Nixon detail. You know, this is after they threw him out of office?"

March nodded. It looked like this could be a long story. He fished a hip flask out of his pocket, took a slug. Offered one to Healy, but come on, of course not.

"Anyway, Nixon's driving around one day, around San Clemente, just him and a few agents…"

"Yeah," March said, brushing a finger across his teeth and straightening his tie. Tally was a classy lady. Needed to make a good impression.

"And they come across this car accident, right? This guy pinned under a car." Healy paused like he was remembering it, this scene he never saw. "Anyway. Nixon gets out, runs over to check on the guy. You know, leans down. And Nixon says to him, 'You're gonna be okay, son. You're gonna be all right.' "

Healy looked up at March, who'd planted a new cigarette between his lips. "And right then…the guy dies."

He seemed to be waiting for March to say something.

"I don't get it," March said, lighting his Camel.

"Think about it from that guy's point of view," Healy

said, "okay? The guy who died. He's lying there on the ground, staring up at the sky, near death, and then former president Richard Nixon appears before him and tells him he's gonna be fine. Now, did he think that's normal? Right? That, before they die, everybody sees Nixon?"

"You're expecting an angel and you get Nixon," March said.

"Exactly. Right."

"Okay," March said.

"The same situation," Healy said, "just a vastly different point of view."

"So, there's two ways to look at something," March said. Did Healy not notice the exasperation in his voice? Because it was there.

"Yeah," Healy said.

"That's the point of the story?"

"Yeah," Healy said.

"Just say that," March said.

"What?"

"Well, you just lead me on this epic fucking journey with this story, and ten minutes later the point is that there's two ways to look at something, just…you can just say that."

Healy stared at him. "You didn't like that story?"

It was The Stare. And March was not currently drunk, hence capable of fear. Healy wouldn't break his other arm over something like this, would he?

March took a long drag on his cigarette.

"That would be awful," he said, and let Healy think he meant the business about Nixon.

"Wouldn't it, right?"

"Yeah," March said.

At that moment Tally came out through the front door. She was wearing a white blazer over an orange shirt and all March could think, looking at it, was that it looked like a sunset over a white sand beach. Could he tell her that or would that just seem weird? At least unprofessional. Probably both, unprofessional and weird. But man, this chick was something else.

"Hey," he said.

"Oh, thank god," Tally said. She came over carrying a small metal suitcase. "One hundred thousand dollars. Packed it myself."

She looked at the two of them, seemed undecided for a second, then handed over the suitcase and a slip of paper with an address on it—to Healy. Huh. Well, Healy was bigger. Good for carrying things. And maybe she wanted March's hands free for, like, a handshake, or a hug or something.

Wait, she was saying something. "—not common that you find such nice people in the world. Thank you." She almost seemed to be tearing up, she was so grateful. Yeah, a hug. But with Healy there…it just felt awkward.

Healy turned and headed toward the car and March started going with him—but then he turned back, for a private sidebar, as the lawyers called it. "I'm sorry about him," March said. "He just…wanted to come along, I don't know why. But—I'll, I'll call you." He made a sign of a telephone with his hand by his ear. "You know, when we make the—the drop."

Tally looked...what? He couldn't put his finger on what that expression meant. He was going to say relieved. Or, like, turned on. Yes, he'd definitely have to call her. Just needed to find her number. But how hard could that be? He was a detective, right?

"Thank you," Tally said again, and he could tell she really meant it.

"You nervous at all?" March asked.

"Me? No." Healy was sitting beside him, staring calmly ahead as the night unrolled before them. The highway was practically empty. They could've been rocketing across the desert, or the surface of the moon. "I've got insurance," Healy told him, and he tugged up his right pants leg to reveal a reinforced leather holster with a handgun tucked away inside it. "This baby right here."

"That an ankle gun?"

"That is an ankle gun, yes."

"Pretty sweet," March said, thinking, I ought to get me one of those.

"Uh-huh," Healy said.

March drove on. He wondered what, exactly, they were driving into. Tally had seemed frightened, and he didn't think she'd be an easy person to frighten. Was her boss a criminal, like Amelia had said? Would Tally know it if she was? And not even like your garden-variety criminal, taking bribes or something, but an actual honest-to-god murderer, several times over. It was hard to swallow, the head of the Justice Department, having her own daughter's friends killed. But, you know, so was Kent State—hard to swallow. And so was JFK. And Bobby, and King, and J. Edgar Hoover and Vietnam and Watergate, and the list went on. This was the US of A, not some tin-pot Third-World shithole where the cops and the government secretly rounded up their own citizens and had them shot, but then again, sometimes it fucking was.

And now he was sounding like Amelia.

March blinked a few times. It had been a long fucking night. He shook his head, hard, to clear it, but it didn't work. His eyelids felt like curtains. "I'm falling asleep at the wheel here, man," he said. "I'm gonna need you to drive. I'm gonna pull over up here."

Healy looked at him like he was the biggest fucking idiot in the world. "You don't have to pull over," he said. "Car can drive itself."

"What?"

"Just take your hands off the wheel, man."

What the fuck was he talking about? But the man looked so confident, so certain. So calm. Did he know something March didn't? It wasn't like he wanted to crash. Hell, he didn't even have his seat belt on. Okay, then. March lifted his hands off the steering wheel.

They didn't crash.

Not only that, the ride felt smoother and more comfortable than ever. He wasn't touching the steering wheel, but it was turning all the same, making minor adjustments to the left and right, like an invisible hand was turning it.

So March lifted his foot off the gas pedal.

And damned if that didn't work the same way. It went down on its own, speeding the car up, without him having to do a thing.

"Hm." March dropped his hands into his lap. This was pretty great. "I didn't know it could do that." He used his free hands to take out a cigarette and light it, all while the car drove itself.

"Where you been, man?" Healy said. "Every car can do this."

"Yeah, March, where the fuck have you been, man?" came a voice from the back seat, accompanied by a loud buzzing noise, and when March turned his head to look, he saw this giant fucking honeybee sitting right behind him, like six feet tall, antennas waving, mandibles clicking, compound eyes gleaming.

"Idiot," the bee said. "You didn't know that?" It raised a cigarette to its own mouth.

"You fly everywhere," March said. "You don't even drive. What do you know?"

"He's got a point there, Bumble," Healy said over his shoulder.

"Yeah, whatever," the bee said. "I used to fly all the time, but now the smog is just disgusting, man, this pollution is out of control. All the bees are riding around in cars these days…"

"Yeah," Healy said, "you better wake up, man."

"What?" March said, and then he realized Healy was shouting: *Wake up! Wake up! March!*

Holy shit—March's eyes shot open to reveal a row of orange traffic cones going flying one by one as the front end of the car plowed into them. Up ahead, the side wall of an overpass was zooming toward them. He grabbed at the steering wheel, tried to turn it, and Healy was grabbing at it too, but they were pulling in opposite directions, so all they both managed to do was steer the car straight ahead. They smashed into the line of hard plastic water barrels at the foot of the overpass, which exploded, showering water everywhere. The rear end of the car fishtailed into the air before landing back down again with a spine-jarring thump. March watched with horror as Tally's metal suitcase, unsecured in the back seat, went flying overhead and struck one of the concrete pilings of the overpass. Better it than them, that was for sure. But the case snapped open under the impact and its contents spilled out, paper raining down all over the goddamn highway. A hundred thousand dollars.

Only it wasn't a hundred thousand dollars.

As the blizzard of paper fluttered over them, March saw white, he saw red, he saw black. He didn't see green. It was like that old joke, what's black and white and red all over? Cut-up newspaper, that's what. Fucking newspaper. Someone had switched out Tally's cash for—

But no, she'd said she'd packed it herself.

"That's not money," Healy said, with his gift for the obvious.

"*Why.*" March pounded his fists on the steering wheel. "Why would she send us off on some wild fucking goose chase?"

Healy looked at him. "Amelia."

35

Amelia was asleep behind the closed door of Holly's bedroom. Holly was cleaning up in the kitchen, having fried up the last of the corned beef and chased it with a batch of Nestlé Toll House cookies, following the recipe on the package. They'd come out a little too hard, but like her dad would say, fuck it. Bad cookies were still cookies and, between them, she and Jessica had eaten them all.

Jessica was on the phone now, with Rosie Milligan, a friend of theirs who never seemed to do anything but loved to hear about everything everyone else did, and consequently spent her whole life on the telephone. Not entirely unlike Jessica.

"No, like *The Waltons*," Jessica was saying. "Yeah, like on TV. Richard something? Yeah. What's that actor's name…?"

"Jessica," Holly said, "get off the phone."

"All *right*," Jessica said, but she turned right back to her call. "Yeah, anyway, so this John-Boy is like a murderer, or something? Uh-huh. The actor. Shit. Now it's going to bug me."

The front doorbell rang, and Holly ran to get it. The man outside was dressed in a three-piece suit, bland and brown, and he carried a doctor's bag in one gloved hand. He smiled down at her. "You must be Holly."

Holly smiled, nodded.

"Dr. Malek," the man said, and he extended one hand for a shake. Did he look like a doctor? Well, Holly supposed so. He was a bit younger than she'd have expected, and a good deal better-looking, though he'd really have been more attractive with a better haircut, and without that huge mole on the side of his face.

"Hi," Holly said. "She's inside. Come in."

They'd managed to get the car untangled from the barrels, raced along the freeway to the nearest exit, hunted down a payphone by the side of an all-night convenience store. Dialed March's number twice. Three times. Each time, a loud busy signal had blared back at them.

March looked at his wristwatch, hammered the gas, and prayed the goddamn car would hold together long enough to get them to his house.

"You mind fetching your dad?" Dr. Malek asked, looking around the March home in a queer sort of way.

"Uh, he's running an errand," Holly said.

"Back any time soon?" Dr. Malek wanted to know.

"Oh, an hour, tops," Holly said.

"Fine," said Dr. Malek. "Now, then—Nurse Holly. How's our patient?" He looked over, saw Jessica on the couch, phone receiver glued to her ear. "That her?"

Holly laughed. "No, that's Jessica. What she's got, you can't fix."

Dr. Malek laughed at that one, like it was the cleverest joke he'd heard in a long time. It was a guffaw, really. "You are *very* funny."

"In there," Holly said, pointing to her bedroom. "Asleep. Slight fever."

"Hm," said Dr. Malek. "On drugs, do you think?" And he gave Holly a little we're-all-grown-ups-here wink. He lifted a thumb and forefinger to his lips, made a toking gesture. "Maybe smoking the reefer?"

It was at that moment that Holly began to doubt this was a real doctor.

He drew closer to her. "What was she saying? Was she...making sense?"

Holly started stammering a response. "She, uh, called us fascists—"

"Hold on," Jessica said into the phone. She took the receiver away from her ear. "Hey, Holly? What's the name of the guy on *The Waltons* who plays John-Boy? With the hockey puck on his face? It's driving me crazy."

Holly froze. The man standing before her was staring. He wasn't blinking. She looked past his ice-blue eyes to the hockey puck on his face.

"That show's for retards," she said weakly. She forced a laugh.

A slight smile bent the man's lips upward just the tiniest little bit, like he knew human beings smiled at times like this and he figured he should do it if he wanted to pass for one. It was chilling.

"Dr. Malek," Holly said, "would you like a cookie? Just baked 'em."

He opened his mouth to answer, but Jessica—back on the telephone—jumped in helpfully: "There's none left. I looked, remember?"

"No," Holly said, her voice rising, insistent, "there's a couple. Doctor…?"

She started edging toward the cookie jar on the counter.

"I could be persuaded," he said, "after I have a look at Sleeping Beauty."

Holly slid the top off the cookie jar, stuck her hand inside, and came up with her father's .38. She pointed it at the son of a bitch in a two-handed grip, just like her dad had taught her.

The man raised his arms up high to either side, like he was being crucified, and shook his head slowly from side to side. "Nurse Holly," he said. He was very disappointed.

He let his doctor's bag drop heavily to the floor.

Jessica finally looked up from the phone. "Holly…! What are you doing? Are you *crazy*?"

But Holly wasn't paying any attention to her friend. Her eyes were focused on the man in front of her. "There are handcuffs behind the bar, asshole," she said. "Get them."

He glanced over at his watch, then back at her. "This is really slowing me down, Holly." His too-friendly fake doctor voice had been replaced by a low growl.

"What's going on?" Jessica cried, dropping the receiver.

"Jessica, it's *him*. He's the guy!"

"Jessica," John-Boy said, calmly, lowering his hands, and reaching into his pocket, "if you help me with this…" He took something out, flicked it open. It was a straight razor. "…I'll only kill Holly."

◦

They were off the highway and rocketing along side streets, March driving maniacally while in the next seat Healy loaded his gun. One of his guns, March corrected himself. There was the ankle gun too. Jesus, he hoped they wouldn't need either of them.

He floored it, tore through a red light.

Go ahead, get on my tail, he thought, *try to give me a ticket. Please.* He'd have welcomed the sight of a cop car, pulling in behind him from a concealed location. Sirens, lights. The more the merrier.

Just don't let us be too late.

"Jessica," Holly said, trying to sound firm and confident, trying to keep panic out of her voice, "dial 911."

"Jessica," John-Boy said, "I wouldn't do that if I were you."

Jessica looked from one of them to the other, like there was a choice here for her to make. Seriously? The killer with a straight razor in his hand or your best friend? Granted, with a gun in hers, but still. A killer or your best friend? A six-foot-something grown man who you know has murdered, what, a dozen people? More? Or your friend? Come on. On the scale of life's little dilemmas, this was an easy one. Get back on the phone, Jessica. It's what you do best. You've been on that goddamn phone all night, you can do it again. It's just lying there on the couch where you dropped it. Just three little numbers, a nine, a one, and a one. Come on, Jessica—

But Jessica was completely frozen.

Outside, some distance away, they heard the sound of a car, engine racing, tires squealing. Holly allowed herself to hope. But this was L.A. That was a sound you heard ten times an hour.

It did seem to break Jessica out of her paralysis, though. Her hand moved toward the telephone.

"Jessica…? I wouldn't do that if I were you," John-Boy repeated sternly.

"Jessica, don't listen!" Holly shouted. "Get help!"

It was too much for her. Some girls just can't handle pressure, Holly knew that. She'd just been hoping Jessica was made of stronger stuff.

Jessica bolted. Which wouldn't have been the worst thing in the world if she'd chosen to run *away* from the killer. But what she did was cross in front of him, trying for the shortest path to the front door. And then his arm was around her waist, and his razor was at her throat.

Holly would've pulled the trigger, but he was holding Jessica in front of him, like a shield. Jesus. "If you hurt her, I swear to god, I'll kill you," Holly said.

But he had something else in mind. He lifted Jessica off her feet and *threw* her at Holly, who dropped to the floor. Jessica passed overhead, arms flailing, screaming as she flew toward the side window and smashed through it. Glass scattered everywhere.

John-Boy raised his razor overhead and took half a step forward—

But now that engine sound was louder, and a pair of headlights blasted through the front window, raking John-Boy's back and blinding Holly as she looked toward the door. *Please let it be them, please let it be them…*

John-Boy was a professional. As much as he would have loved to slice up this little bitch who'd caused him no end of trouble, he had a job to do, and he never let personal pleasure interfere with getting his work done. He turned on his heel and in two steps was out of the house, razor tucked away in his pocket for another time.

"You hear that?" March asked, as he and Healy jumped out of the car. It had sounded like breaking glass.

There was a man in a brown suit walking calmly, casually, from their front door to a gold sedan parked by the curb.

"Excuse me," March called to him.

"Evening," the fellow called back, raising one hand to wave and smiling a little stiffly.

"You hear that sound just a second ago?"

"Oh yeah, just now." The man was at the trunk of his car, unlocking it with his keys. "That was me. I threw that little girl out the window." And without missing a beat he reached into the trunk, drew out a Sterling submachine gun, and started firing in their direction.

Healy and March dropped to the ground as bullets started flying their way. The car was peppered, reduced within seconds to an undriveable wreck.

Well, at least it had gotten them home.

"Cover me," March said, the killer's words echoing in his ears: *I threw that little girl out the window*. Was it terrible that he was hoping he meant the *other* little girl? Nah. He was entitled.

Healy whipped out his gun and popped up above the car door, took two shots at John-Boy, then a third. Didn't hit him, that was too much to hope for, but the machine gun stopped firing as the assassin ducked behind a tree, and March used the brief respite to run across the street, crouching, praying, making himself as small a target as he possibly could. He heard Healy firing again as he made it to the far side. *Thank you*.

And thank you again—this one for the big guy, since the girl lying in the shrubs below the side window was a) alive, and b) not his daughter. She was groaning and covered with glass. But she'd live. He hefted her onto his shoulder, in a sort of half-assed fireman's carry, and ran with her toward the door. "Holly!" he shouted. "Holly!"

From inside, Holly shouted back: "Dad!"

"Get in! Get down!" March threw the door open and carried Jessica through the living room and on into Holly's bedroom.

Back on the street, Healy was running for the door, too. Only he was doing it without any covering fire but his own. March chanced a look back. The crazy bastard. Why didn't he just stay by the car?

"Is she okay?" Holly asked, and it took him a second to realize she meant Jessica.

"She's fine," March told her. "Now come on."

The machine gun fire had resumed, and it was tearing up the street, the trees, the neighboring houses. Healy was sheltering behind a concrete planter, planning his next move. This was like fucking D-Day, like his dad on Omaha Beach. He was remembering the stories the old man had told him on his rare visits home, about taking territory one bloody yard at a time. He'd wanted those stories when he'd been seven and eight and nine, couldn't get enough of them, but then he had outgrown the heroic bullshit when he'd hit his teens. And that's when his dad had told him, at the end of one particularly difficult conversation, that it wasn't about being a hero, none of it was, son, it was just about staying alive. One more day, one more hour, one more minute. You were alive or you were dead, those were the options, and if you survived one minute, that just bought you the chance to try for another. And another. That's what war is, and that's what life is: getting to the next minute. And Healy had called him a coward, because it's the word he figured would hurt the old man the most, and because he was angry, and four months later he was picking avocados and trying to make sense of Thomas Aquinas.

But the old man had been right, of course. When pinned down under fire, you have one job and only one job, and that's to stay alive.

So Healy did his job. He crouched, he popped his hand up over the planter's edge, he fired two more times in John-Boy's direction, and then he ran, hell for leather, chased every step of the way by gunfire, until he could drop to a squat behind the dense trunks of a cluster of palms. And reload. And hope March had gotten the girls out of the line of fire.

✿

Which March had—for now. He had put Holly and Jessica
(still unconscious, and maybe that was just as well) in
the large bedroom closet, sitting on the floor, then he'd
jumped a good three feet in the air when Amelia had
popped up out of the bathroom and shouted, "Fucking
fascists!"

"Jesus!" March screamed.

"Sorry," Amelia said. "Didn't know it was you."

"Get in there," he said, pointing to the closet, and
Amelia meekly followed. Well, okay. That was better.

"Come here," he said to Holly, and drew her into a
quick, desperate hug. "Now, stay in there and don't move.
Okay?" He closed the closet door.

"Wait, dad, wait," came Holly's voice, "Here." The door
opened and his own gun poked out at him.

"Jeez," March shouted, stumbling back again, away
from the wildly waving firearm. Then he grabbed it from
her. Good girl. He headed for the door. Couldn't believe
that's what he was doing, but there were his feet, and
they were carrying him toward, not away from, the sound
of gunfire. Will wonders never cease.

Right about then, Healy was wondering whether the gunfire would ever cease. Didn't seem likely, unless he ran
out of bullets himself. Which—he calculated in his head—
wasn't so far off. Damn it. He rose up, shot once, dropped
back down. He had to start conserving ammo.

Then he heard shots coming from the direction of the
house—one, two, three—and saw a row of bullet holes

spring up along John-Boy's open trunk. March! Healy saw John-Boy's head swivel, take in the sight of March sheltering behind the door jamb, gun raised. The killer didn't miss a beat, just reached into the trunk with his free hand and came back up with a second gun. Now he was firing two-handed, the submachine gun aimed at Healy, a tight little black handgun aimed at March. Holy shit.

March ducked back into the house as the wood splintered where his face had just been. Healy ducked as well, then heard an ominous creaking sound overhead. He looked up—then jumped to his feet and started fucking running.

In the closet, Jessica stirred. Holly felt her friend's head move against her shoulder. "Jessica!" She turned to Amelia, "I think she's awake." Then she realized that Amelia wasn't sitting next to her anymore, she was standing with her hand on the closet door. "Wait, where are you going?"

Next to Holly, Jessica moaned.

"It's okay," Holly said. "You're okay."

From outside, the noise of the gunfight continued. Holly turned back to Amelia.

But Amelia wasn't there. She'd left the closet and was heading toward Holly's bedroom window.

"What are you doing?" Holly shouted.

Amelia was up on the sill now, then she had the window open and one leg out. She called back, "Tell Mr. Healy thanks for nothing." And she dropped out of sight.

In a quiet instant between gunshots, Holly heard Amelia's desperate footsteps pattering away.

o

There's cover and there's cover. Healy's cover in this case
came in the form of one of the palm trees, which, having
been raked across the trunk repeatedly by machine gun
fire, had finally had enough and decided it was time to lie
down. The whole fucking thing started tilting, and then
falling, and Healy ran behind it as it fell, all the way to the
house. As the tree crashed down with a colossal roar of
snapping fronds, Healy put his arms up in front of his
face and hurtled through the big kitchen window in an
explosion of glass. He rolled when he hit the floor, scrambled, came to a rest with his back against the wall, head
just below window level. He was feeling around his jacket
desperately for his last spare magazine as March came
around the corner.

"You okay?" March said.

"March! Gun! Gun!"

Give the man credit—he sized the situation up at a
glance. Professional killer outside, still firing, partner on
the ground, empty gun in his hands, fumbling for a fresh
magazine he didn't even know if he still had. March didn't
hesitate, he threw his handgun in Healy's direction.

It flew over Healy's shoulder and out the shattered
window.

"Fuck!" Healy shouted.

"Shit!" was March's opinion.

And from outside John-Boy chimed in with an opinion
of his own, in the form of a fusillade from the Sterling.

March whipped the cookie jar off the kitchen counter
and dropped to the floor beside Healy. He upended it

between them, spilling a shitload of assorted random bullets on the floor, along with a tiny snub-nosed revolver, a crazy little thing he'd taken off a hooker years ago. It was, unfortunately, not loaded. Healy grabbed a handful of bullets and tried to jam them into the chambers.

Then, in the far-off distance, they heard the sounds of sirens.

Well, all right. Finally. It had only taken a thousand rounds before the LAPD had woken up.

The machine gun fire ceased. Sticking his head up over the windowsill, Healy saw John-Boy toss the Sterling in his car, slam the trunk shut, and jump behind the wheel. Healy fired twice—all he could, he'd only found two bullets that fit—and both shots hit home, but they only starred the windshield glass. John-Boy didn't even look perturbed. He just calmly pulled out and drove off, his red taillights vanishing down the road.

The silence that followed—broken only by the rising and falling wail of the approaching sirens—was blissful.

"He's gone," March said, and he ran for Holly's bedroom. "He's gone!"

Holly was there, and Jessica, awake now and sitting miserably in an armchair, cradling her head in her hands. And Amelia…?

Where was Amelia?

Holly pointed toward the bedroom window.

Amelia was in the woods. Still barefoot, frightened as hell, chilly in that little yellow dress, arms wrapped around her own chest for warmth or maybe just reassurance. She stumbled from tree to tree, keeping the gunfire behind her.

The highway. She'd make for the highway. Someone would stop, someone would have to. And then she'd get away. Lie low. Give a fake name, she'd done it before, she could do it again. She'd been Harriet once, and Francie, and Faith, and oh, god, so many other names. She'd worked off the books packing boxes in a warehouse and cleaning floors in an illegal rehab clinic. She'd hooked, too, but fuck it, who hadn't. She'd gotten by, was the point. She'd survived. She'd do it again.

At some point, she realized the gunfire had ended, or maybe she'd just made it far enough that she could no longer hear it. No, it must've stopped. That was one thing about gunshots, you could hear them a long, long way off.

Well, good. Maybe Healy had gotten lucky and taken that prick out. She could hope.

But even if he had, her mother would send another. And another. Unless she took her down first. Which—

It was still possible. The bitch didn't know it, but it was still possible, and more than possible. It was *going* to happen. Yes, it was. She just had to stay alive long enough and she'd get to enjoy seeing it happen, seeing her mother's face on the nightly news, seeing Walter fucking Cronkite read the headline over a clip of her mommy being led away in handcuffs. God, that would feel so good.

Amelia stepped out from between two trees when she heard—finally—a car coming along the road. Not racing or anything, just driving, and that was good because it meant the driver would see her and have time to react and stop. And the car *would* stop. She was a pretty, young girl in a little yellow dress, bruised and bloody and barefoot, what kind of asshole wouldn't stop for her?

She held her arms up, waved them over her head, and the car slowed. She couldn't see anything beyond the bright, bright headlights, but the point was, the car was stopping. Even if it was a creep, even if it was some asshole who'd make her blow him in return for taking her out of the state, that was okay, she'd do it. Just as long as he got her to safety, right?

She ran up to the door, and the driver leaned over toward her and cranked down the passenger-side window.

"Please, I need to get out of here," she began, and then John-Boy shot her in the chest.

Her body crumpled to the ground.

John-Boy smiled and drove off.

36.

They were on a bench outside the courthouse, not far from where they'd watched the protest group hold their die-in on the City Hall steps. It was a beautiful day.

March was scratching under the edge of his cast, not because his arm itched, just fucking because. He was looking down at his hands. Healy, sitting next to him, was staring straight ahead. By Healy's side was a newspaper, discarded. Amelia's death hadn't made the front page. Not with the multiple killings at the Burbank Airport Western to cover—that was national news. *Richard "Rocco" Sicorio fell fifteen stories to the ground-floor parking lot, although investigators also reported finding multiple gunshot wounds to his torso, any one of which could have been the cause of death…*

Amelia was on page four.

Healy had closed the paper and set it face down. He and March had said everything there was to say to each other, two or three times at least, and now they were just sitting there, waiting.

Perry eventually came out of the building and they got up off the bench to join him.

Perry was their lawyer.

"She had her fucking daughter killed, Perry," March said, "please tell me they're at least gonna question her."

Perry showed what he thought of that idea with a single curl of his lip. "They haven't, and they're not going to."

"Because…?" Healy said.

"Because she's the head of the Justice Department." Perry wheeled on them both, stopped walking. He had a point to make. "Oh, and by the way? You're welcome. You're out, free. On your own recognizance. You get to walk. There should be like a statue of me in your fucking house."

March was lighting a cigarette and trying hard not to care. About any of it.

"I'm sorry, guys," Perry said. "You're going to lose this one. All right? Your word against hers, no evidence, you lose." He shook his head at them both. "You better seriously think about changing your story."

Holly was standing by the open rear door of a taxi. She gave them a little wave as they came down the steps to her.

March waved back half-heartedly.

The ride back to the March homestead was bumper-to-bumper, giving them all plenty of time to think things through.

In the front seat beside the driver, Holly looked out the windshield and tried to imagine what her mother would've said at a time like this. It wasn't hard. She'd loved dad, loved him more the less he deserved it, loved him when he'd fucked around on her and when he'd stayed out late and come home barely able to stand. She would've said, in her beautiful, beautiful, polished and plummy Belvedere accent, "Fuck them, Holl. Fuck them. Stand up to them and tell them they're fucking wrong." She was a believer in absolutes. And one of her absolutes was Holland March.

Holly looked out at the birds winging in a flock through the sky and practiced not crying.

Healy was looking at the birds, too, and thinking maybe being a private eye wasn't all it was cracked up to be. Strangely—paradoxically, you might even say, if you had a good calendar to tell you what the word meant—people didn't hate a knee-breaker the way they hated a detective. Breaking someone's knees, or arm, or jaw, was a good, honest profession, and by and large the people you did it to knew why it was being done, and they accepted it. They knew they owed money. They knew Kitten was underage. They knew it, and they took their punishment. But the people a private eye went after—those people fought back, and they fought dirty. Now, maybe that was all the more reason to go into the business of putting them away. Wasn't it better to stand up to the powerful than to beat down little people who didn't expect any better? And Healy was prepared to say that, yes, it was. But like that day at the diner, did he have to be the one to do it? Just this once, couldn't someone else stand up and take the bullet in the arm?

And March was watching the birds, too. He'd struggled out of his jacket and balled it up under his head and meant to try to sleep some, but sleep just wasn't coming— all the start-and-stop of L.A. traffic. And with sleep out of the question, he'd started thinking about why he'd gone into this line of work in the first place, not meaning the private work, but when he'd joined the force. He'd been an idealist, right? At one point? He could hardly remember. But yeah, at one point he must've been. And then had come the hard lessons at the hands of older cops, the grifts and grafts, the corners cut and compromises made. And it's not like the seeds hadn't landed on fertile ground in Holland March's case. Oh, he'd been ready, and in no time at all he'd had his eyes closed and his hand out like a good boy. Thin blue line, fuck, it was a thick blue line in L.A. and getting thicker every day. And yet—

And yet.

"Ah, fuck it," he said, watching the birds wheeling through the sky. "Maybe they're right. Maybe the goddamn birds can't breathe."

Beside him, Healy was nodding.

"Amelia…Misty…Dean…Shattuck," Healy said, "all dead. The rest of us just get to choke."

Holly sighed deeply. "I need a drink," she said.

37

While Healy paid off the cabbie, Holly and her father got out and stared at the wreckage of their house. Rented house, it was true. But still the second home they'd lost in the course of one year. Would a flood be next? A plague of locusts? Maybe they'd get whipped up in a tornado like in that old movie and wind up in the land of Oz, dancing around with the Lollipop Guild.

"I always hated that palm tree," Holly said, staring at it as it lay, placidly, with its trunk sprawled across the roof.

"Never trusted it," March said.

"Yeah."

"Go inside and get your stuff," he told her. "We'll go stay in a hotel or something."

"Okay." Holly headed off, ducked under the yellow tape that said *CRIME SCENE DO NOT CROSS* over and over.

"We'll get room service," March called.

Behind him, he heard the sound of a car pulling in and thought maybe the cab had come back, maybe they'd left something in the back seat. But turning around he saw it was a two-tone Oldsmobile, a clunker whose undercarriage was dragging against the pavement and whose driver was in similar condition. Before he saw her face, March saw her support hose emerge, and then the giant batik handbag, which landed in the driveway by her feet.

With a groan, Lily Glenn dragged herself out of the seat

and hobbled over to where the two men were standing. She peered at March through her thick, round lenses.

"*Mister* March," she said, and she did not sound pleased.

"Mrs. Glenn," March said.

"I need to talk to you," she intoned.

"What a, what a wonderful surprise," March said, with what he thought must be the worst fake smile he'd ever mustered.

Mrs. Glenn peered past him at the fallen tree, the shattered windows. "That your house…?"

"We're remodeling," March said. "Listen, this isn't a great time—"

"It is a *great* time," she insisted. She walked over to Healy. "He is supposed to be looking for my niece."

Healy stared at March. "Is he really."

March pretended he hadn't heard.

"I thought he quit," Healy said.

"Oh, he did," Mrs. Glenn said, "he tried. But I insisted he continue. Because I *saw* her." Her voice rose. "But nobody believes me. Why will nobody believe me?"

Behind her, March was making gestures—a finger rotating beside his ear like a pencil sharpener, a finger across his throat.

"I'm sure I don't know, ma'am," Healy said.

"I *saw* her," Mrs. Glenn said, "in her house, through the front window, as clear as day. Writing something, at a desk. She was wearing a blue pinstripe jacket."

"I've seen that jacket, sure," Healy said.

March stopped gesturing. "What do you mean you saw that jacket?"

"In Shattuck's place, this storage room, with a bunch of other clothes."

"That jacket was in Sid Shattuck's place?"

"Yeah," Healy said, "the whole suit. It was bagged up, had Misty's name on it and the name of the movie."

March's eyes lit up. It was the illumination of a circuit suddenly closing. You could almost literally see the light-bulb go on.

"It's wardrobe for the film," he said. "It's *wardrobe* for the *film!*"

So? Healy wasn't sure why that was such an exciting bit of news. So it was wardrobe for the film. So what? It meant the old lady hadn't been imagining things when she described what she saw her niece wearing, but what it meant beyond that Healy couldn't grasp.

But March clearly had something in mind. "Holy fucking shit," he said.

"Oh!" Mrs. Glenn exclaimed, and wagged an outraged finger in his face.

"Sorry," March said, then took hold of her arm and started marching her back to her car. "Mrs. Glenn, I need you to take us to Misty's house, I need you to show us exactly what you saw."

They drove up a steep hill to a little place with white walls and a red door, raised over a garage it shared with the house next door. Wrought-iron railings out front, bay window, some planters on the wall. It wasn't a mansion, that was for sure. Most of the profits from her films had gone to Shattuck, clearly. But it was a decent place to live, in a decent neighborhood. March wondered how many of Misty's neighbors had known how she paid her mortgage.

"There—there," Mrs. Glenn said, pointing, "that's the window. I was coming around that corner, and I saw her, through that window, writing on her desk against the far wall."

They all got out, filed up the stairs and into the house, March first, then Healy, then Holly, and finally, slowly, Mrs. Glenn. One by one they all spotted the same thing. Mrs. Glenn was the one to put it into words.

"But—no—it was here, the desk was here!"

She was standing by a bare wall.

"No desk there now," Healy said.

"Well…I don't know what to say…"

"Dad, what are you doing?" Holly was staring at her father's backside as he crawled around on all fours, poking at what looked like a bulky wooden coffee table in the middle of the room. Actually, it didn't look quite like a coffee table—it was too high and blocky and it had a strange seam down the middle, almost like a dining room table that you could expand by pulling it open and inserting extra leaves. But it didn't quite look like that either.

"Give me a second," March said, grunting, pressing with his fingertips against the base of the unit. Finally he found something, a latch, and pulled it. The two halves of the unit slid apart at the seam, and from underneath a piece of equipment rose into view.

It was a film projector.

"World's worst detective, huh?" He stared at Holly,

who had her arms crossed again. Her favorite pose. But she was going to have to eat her words.

"You *did* see your niece, Mrs. Glenn," March said exultantly. "You saw her on that wall, at a desk, in a pinstripe suit."

"So, what she saw through the window," Healy said, slowly, remembering his own recent encounter with a projection system that threw the image of a beautiful woman, large as life, on the wall of a room, "was a movie."

"Not *a* movie," March said. "*The* movie. *The* movie!"

"But the film burned up," Healy said.

"Well, how did she see it two days after it supposedly burned up? And the wardrobe matches perfectly?"

"So Amelia had a second print?" Healy said. "She had a copy?"

"Wouldn't you?" March said.

Holly spoke up. "And she gave that copy to Misty. So after Misty dies…she comes here to get it…checks the film against that wall…"

"Lily sees it through that window," March said, pointing.

"…and Lily starts knocking on the glass, so Amelia splits. And takes the film."

"And goes…where?" Healy said—but then realized he knew the answer. "The Western Hotel. To meet the businessmen. Didn't you say that Rocco guy was a—"

"Distributor," March said, and he threw his hands up. "Distributors! She was screening it for the distributors! It's out there, the film exists, now we just have to find it."

Holly, meanwhile, was poking around the movie projector. There was no film threaded on it, no film anywhere inside the cabinet it came out of. But she did find a slip of paper.

"Hey, look," she said, and read aloud: " 'Opening night, nine PM.' Signed, Chet."

"Fucking Chet," March said.

"The protestor guy?" Healy said.

"Give me that shit," March said, and took the slip from Holly. He read it over again. "She was planning something with Chet. 'Opening night.' What's opening around now that they would care about…?"

"The L.A. Auto Show," Holly said. "It's today, right? It's been all over the radio."

"Yeah," Healy said. "Big party, mucky-mucks, loads of press. If you wanted to get a story out there…"

"And fucking Chet's a projectionalist ," March said.

"Please!" Mrs. Glenn was standing there, on the verge of tears. "Please, stop talking. I've been listening to everything you've said—does this mean, does this mean…that my niece is dead?"

"Yes!" March exploded. Holly and Healy looked at him. Jesus. He lowered his voice. "I mean, you know, yes? She was murdered. Yeah. I'm sorry."

"But we're going to bring down the people who did it," Holly said, firmly.

"Yeah," March said, nodding sincerely. "And for a deeply discounted rate."

38.

There were hotels and hotels. Compared to this one, the Burbank Airport Western was a doll house. Two glass towers, connected by an elevated walkway, rose at least thirty stories in the air. At their foot, an enormous swimming pool glowed turquoise in the beams of giant searchlights, the sort they'd have at a movie premiere. And it was a premiere—only the stars in this case were the two-ton vehicles rotating majestically on turntables with beautiful women beside them to add to their luster.

"Welcome to Los Angeles, and the 1978 Pacific Coast Auto Show!" an announcer's voice boomed from loudspeakers set up all over the grounds, while on a screen three stories high a projected image showed smiling people enjoying next year's finest cars. WOOD GRAIN PANELING read one caption. And: RECLINING FABRIC SEATS. And: CARPETED DOOR PANELS. And: STYLED ROAD WHEELS.

March led the way through the main pavilion and into the lobby of the near tower, Healy following close on his heels and Holly playing caboose. March hadn't wanted to bring her at first, but she'd put her foot down, and, well, fuck it, he figured she'd earned it if that's what she wanted. Anyway, who could say she'd be safer by herself somewhere? That had almost ended terribly the last time.

After asking at the desk, they rode an elevator up to the ninth floor and found their way to a central atrium. They passed a group of long-haired young men who'd tried to clean up and look more Establishment, but only succeeded in looking like hippies in shoplifted duds. Two were wearing pink suit jackets and the third had on cream over a beige bowtie. They were all taking a cigarette break.

"You guys know where the projection room is?" March asked, figuring these guys for Chet's peer group.

One of them, the porkiest, aimed a thumb toward a nearby hallway.

"You seen Chet, the projectionist?"

"He just left," the porky guy said, "like ten minutes ago, went for a drink. And you are…?"

"In a hurry," March answered, and headed down the hallway. "Thanks, buddy."

"How'd you know my name was Buddy?" the guy called after him.

But March was past answering. He continued till they got to a locked door marked "STAFF ONLY—DO NOT ENTER." This had to be it. It was at the end of the hall, and would have a view out the window to the courtyard below. From the hallway window, they could see the projected image currently on display. It showed a car and a man standing before it—Bergen Paulsen, auto industry spokesman—reciting its virtues for the assembled crowds. March couldn't hear what he was saying through the sealed window, but he assumed the car could not only drive itself but make you a cocktail while you rode. Cars of the future always seemed to do things like that.

"We've got to get in there," March said, and turning back from the window discovered that Healy already had the lock open. He was rising from one knee and slipping a lockpick back into his pocket. Well. That was handy, certainly.

March suggested that Holly stay outside and keep watch, maybe from around that corner there? Holly nodded and took up the position. Healy, meanwhile, had opened the door and gone in.

Inside, they found two projectors set up, both aimed at the open glass doors to the terrace. One projector was running, the footage of Paulsen and his cocktail-making car, and the other had a film queued up to run. Healy ran to that one and unspooled a length, held it up to the light. He just saw frame after frame of—

"It's just a bunch of cars." He squinted to read some type in one run of frames. " '*Motor City Pride.*' That's not it. It's not the film."

"Shit," March said. He picked up a few film cans he saw lying on a table, but they were all empty. "Fucking Chet. He's probably still got it stashed somewhere." He kicked the leg of the table and one of the film cans clattered to the ground.

The noise covered the sound of the hotel room door unlatching again, and neither of them noticed that someone had come in until they heard the click of a hammer arming a handgun.

They turned, saw Tally kick the door shut behind her.

"Tally!" March said. She was dressed in the most stunning coral dress, gold belt, dangling metal earrings, and she'd done something with her hair—it was no longer pinned back, now it was a luxuriant afro. "My god, you look incredible. How do you get your hair to…? It's magnificent."

She waved the gun at him and he put his hands up.

"Listen," March said, "I don't know what's going on here, but there's been some foul play. Do you know that that suitcase that you gave us, somebody switched it out? There was no money it."

Healy saw Tally's eyes roll and felt his own going as well.

"No shit," Tally said, in a no-nonsense voice—a no-more-nonsense voice, to be specific. "Weapons on the floor. Now."

Healy reached into his jacket, got his gun out and tossed it on the floor. March reluctantly threw his away too.

"I guess you killed the projectionist, huh?" Healy said.

"No," Tally said, "my associate is out looking for him now. We'll find him."

Healy gave her a serious look, spoke softly. "Tally, let me ask you something. You ever really killed anybody?"

"In Detroit, yeah. Three times."

"Really?" So much for that approach.

"That's where this all started," Tally said. "The Detroit show. That bitch, Misty, shooting her mouth off about her new movie. All the stir it would cause."

"Tally…this is not you," March said. "You're not a murderer."

"She just said she killed three people," Healy reminded him.

"I know," March said, "but I'm saying deep down." He pointed to his heart, to show how deep down he meant.

"Hey, look, one's a mistake," Healy said, "but, I mean, three, you're a murderer."

"Don't paint her with that brush," March said. "It's easy to live in your world, right, where everyone fits in their place, you pigeonhole people—"

"See what's in front of you," Healy begged him, "she's got a gun."

"You just paint everyone with that brush."

"She's killed three people. Come on, man."

"You don't know her upbringing, you don't know why she…"

"No, I'm just telling you—"

There was a hammering at the door. A low voice called out, "Room service."

Well, not a low voice. A high voice, but trying to sound low, like a little girl might.

Tally was momentarily distracted, and March seized the opportunity to drop to the ground and start fumbling with the leg of Healy's pants. He was patting Healy's right calf, his shin. Nothing. He started pawing Healy's left leg, feeling all around.

"Shit!" Healy said. He threw one hand up as Tally turned back and brought her gun up again. "No!"

"What's wrong with him?" she demanded.

"I…I don't know," Healy said. "I'm gonna ask him. March…?"

"Yeah," March said. He had his hand up inside Healy's pants, was reaching up as far as he could go.

"Uh…what the fuck are you doing?"

"Did you move it?" March asked. He was pawing Healy's thighs now, desperate.

"Move what?"

"The fucking gun!"

"What gun?"

"The fucking ankle gun!"

"Who told you I had an ankle gun?" Healy asked.

"You did! In the car, before we crashed! You were like, oh, check out my ankle gun, you slide your pants up, you show me your ankle gun…"

Healy just looked confused. Tally looked confused and slightly disgusted.

"Come on, are you serious?" Healy said. He was starting to look a little disgusted, too. "You fucking serious?"

"Oh, shit," March said, realizing, "did I dream that?"

"Yeah," Healy said. "Yeah, you moron, you dreamt it."

March raised one finger. He was still thinking it through. "No…no…" Then: "Yeah, I think you're right."

"Shut up!" Tally waved the gun at them. "Just shut up, both of you."

The hammering came at the door again. "Room service!"

Tally kept the gun on them as she stepped back and threw the door open. "Holly? You can come in now."

And Holly did. Wheeling a room service cart. Plates, glasses, a candle, a thermos carafe of coffee.

Tally laughed. "Very clever, Holly."

"Thanks," Holly said, "I thought so." She grabbed the

carafe and hurled its contents in Tally's direction. She was drenched in coffee.

But it didn't have the desired effect.

"Why did you just throw cold coffee on me?" Tally asked her.

"I got it in the hallway," Holly said, sheepishly. "I thought it was hot."

From where he lay, sprawled on the floor at Healy's feet, March piped up. "I like where your head's at, sweetheart. That really could've worked out."

"All right: everybody, in the corner," Tally ordered and strode toward them. One of her platform shoes slid on the slick of cold coffee puddled on the floor beneath her, and then her legs were going out from under her and she landed flat on her back, a little like Amelia had when she'd flown backward off the hood of their car. And with a similar result: her head struck the edge of a table on the way down, and though her finger tightened reflexively on the trigger, shooting a bullet and shattering a light fixture, Tally was unconscious when she hit the ground.

March sprang to his feet. "Well." He straightened his jacket. "That really worked out."

"Yeah," Healy said. He picked up his own gun and grabbed Tally's while he was at it.

March slid his back into his holster. "Now we just have to find fucking Chet before John-Boy does."

"Yeah," Healy said again. "Well, that guy said he was going for a drink. You take the roof bar, I'll take downstairs." He patted Holly on the arm. She was still trembling. "Well done, kiddo."

He headed for the door.

March was tucking a pillow under Tally's head. He took a second to pet her hair. Holly stared at him.

"No reason she has to be uncomfortable."

"Right," Holly said.

He got up and made for the elevators.

39

Upstairs, downstairs.

Like that TV show his wife had hated, saying it didn't reflect Brits well, even though it was made by Brits, wasn't it? Yes, it was, she conceded; but was every TV show made by Americans a good reflection of America? March didn't have to answer that one. The fifties hadn't really been like *Happy Days*, that was for sure. And probably the thirties hadn't been like *The Waltons*.

Speaking of which.

March scanned the portion of the upstairs lounge area he could see from the entry hall by the elevators, half hoping he'd spot the son of a bitch, half hoping he wouldn't. In any event he didn't. He hoped Healy was having better luck downstairs. Worse luck. Whatever.

He turned to Holly. "Just wait here. I'm going to take a look around."

"I want to help!"

"You can help by staying put," he said, and she crossed her arms in a huff.

"Promise me you'll get the film?" Holly said.

"Yeah, sure, I promise," March said, gazing around, trying to notice faces. It was crowded. John-Boy *could* be up here somewhere.

"Pinky promise?" Holly asked, holding up the relevant digit, already crooked for him to take it.

He hesitated, but there was no saying no to that face. He linked fingers with her. "Pinky promise."

She smiled, satisfied. Her dad might break his vows to anyone else—everyone else—but not a pinky promise to her.

"Fuck," March muttered under his breath, and headed off, scanning the crowd to either side of him.

"Hey, pal," a voice called as he passed one bar, "what can I do you for?" The man behind the counter, a bullet-headed bartender in formal vest, black tie and shirt sleeves, waited for his answer.

March did his best Jackson Healy impression and turned him down with a wave. He was working, there were killers on the loose, he needed to keep his wits about him.

The bartender came right back at him: "Free drinks. What are you having?"

Well, *free* drinks. He supposed one wouldn't hurt.

Hell, you never knew, the bartender might know something.

Downstairs, Healy had missed by no more than ten minutes a scene that the bartender down there was now describing to him. Yes, a man had come by, a tall, good looking man with a bad haircut and a big mole on the side of his face. Yes, he'd been looking for Chet. Yes, he'd found him.

"You the projectionist?" he'd said, or words to that effect—the bartender hadn't been paying too close attention, understand?

Healy understood.

Chet had swallowed a good mouthful of his drink before responding, a Manhattan, as the bartender recalled—no, a Rob Roy, that was it, a dry Rob Roy, he remembered the kid had been very particular about it, like he knew fuck-all about cocktails at whatever he was, eighteen? If that. For heaven's sake, did you know what your drink was at eighteen…?

Healy had been kind of partial to all of them, actually. But that wasn't the point right now. He tried to steer the bartender back: So, the kid had gone with the tall man…?

Well, not at first—he had half his drink left, remember. But the tall man had gotten into it with him, saying stuff like "We have a problem on nine" and "Someone knocked over the projector, the film's all over the floor." The kid had gone, "Film's on the floor, really?" and the tall man was like, "Yeah. It's a mess."

And *then* the kid had gone with him…?

Well, he took one more swallow of his drink first, his dry Rob Roy, but then, yeah, he'd gotten up and followed the big guy.

Which way?

The bartender pointed—and Healy pounded off, right through the side door he was indicating.

It was a service door, and behind it Healy found a loading dock full of wooden pallets stored on end and metal galley racks waiting for kitchen trays to fill them up. A blustery union man sitting with half his capacious ass on a stool (*Capacious*, adjective: large in capacity, spacious) pointed him toward the far end of the dock.

Healy jogged down to that end, peering into the shadows, calling out, "Hey, Chet? Chet?"

He heard a groan in response, muffled, as if the person doing the groaning was covered under a pile of laundry or something. It turned out to be a pile of garbage, heaped high in a dumpster by one wall. The groaning got louder as Healy approached. He tossed broken-down cardboard boxes to either side and some leftovers from the evening's kitchen prep: wilted lettuce leaves, carrot peelings, onion skins. Halfway down he found Chet, his face a bloody mass of bruises and broken bones.

"Hey—hey, Chet?"

"Uhhh," the kid moaned. His eyes were closed. Closed, hell—they were swollen shut. Healy had seen fighters who'd gone a dozen rounds that looked better than this kid. Losing fighters.

But then they'd fought in their own weight class.

"Amelia's film," Healy said, feeling lousy about pressing, but figuring he didn't have much time—not just because John-Boy was on the move again, also because this kid didn't look like he had more than a sentence left in him. "Where is it?"

The kid told him.

It only took a sentence.

Which was just as well, since he was dead by the end of it.

John-Boy's voice came out of the walkie-talkie, and just hearing it again made Holly's skin crawl. She sat up straighter and listened. "The film is in the projector,"

John-Boy said, his voice low and crackling with static. "Repeat: in the projector."

"We already checked that," came the response, and this voice Mr. Healy would've recognized, and maybe her dad, but Holly did not. She peered over her shoulder, trying to make it look casual as she did so. The guy speaking into the walkie-talkie was older than her dad, older than Healy, but not *old* old—just a regular-looking older guy, black, wearing a red three-piece suit, and walking around with a limp, like maybe he'd injured his leg sometime recently.

John-Boy was talking again: "It's spliced into the middle, right in the other film."

"Tell Tally, she's the closest."

The voice crackled from the speaker. "She's not answering."

"On my way," said the older man, sounding concerned. As he flicked off the walkie-talkie, he spied Holly looking at him. She turned away, bent her head forward, imagined herself a turtle huddling inside its shell. Maybe he hadn't actually seen her—she could hope. And if he had, maybe it wouldn't mean anything to him. She was just a girl who'd noticed a guy talking into a walkie-talkie, that's all. There was no reason he'd recognize her. People always said she looked nothing like her dad.

When nothing happened for a minute, she began to relax.

Then a voice whispered at her ear. "Don't you know it's rude to eavesdrop?"

✷

Sadly, the bartender hadn't known anything other than how to keep pouring piña coladas. But he'd done that skillfully and March was now thoroughly lubricated. Maybe that's why he didn't show any reaction at all when the guy in the red suit sidled up behind him and said, "I've got a gun pointed directly at your daughter's spine."

"A gun…? Why's that?" March said. He looked up, saw the two of them in the mirror behind the bar, Holly in front looking downcast, the black guy behind her in his Santa suit—or was it Satan? Someone who dressed all in red, anyway. "Hey, Holly, your buddy here wan' a drink? They're free."

"Mr. March," said Red Suit, "I want to know what you and your friend did with Tally—"

March spun on his stool to face them. Holly's heart fell when she realized he was smashed. Absolutely smashed.

"Squee-dap!" March squeezed his eyes shut and sang, a poor echo of the jazzy melody playing over the bar's loudspeakers. "Boo-do-bup-ba! Bippity boo dat boo… How does that song go?"

Holly sighed in disgust.

"Get up," the man said. "Right now. We're taking a walk."

March alit from the stool, teetered a little when he landed. "Lead the way, Santa baby."

"No," the man said, "you lead." He prodded Holly in the back with his gun. She took her father's arm and fought to keep him upright as they walked toward the other side of the roof. The empty side.

"Where we goin'?" March said with a grin. "We gonna watch the birds…?"

The man cocked his gun. "We're gonna clear your head. One way or another."

Down on the ninth floor, in the projection room, a little device with a numbered dial on the front clicked and the dial rotated one step counter-clockwise. There was a notch on the dial above the number zero, and above that, on a metal ring surrounding the dial, there was a red arrow, pointing downward at the top like the flapper on a wheel of fortune. The notch had been two clicks away from the arrow. It was now just one click away. Deep in the guts of this little device, an even littler motor was humming away.

A wire ran from the base of the device along the floor past where Tally lay, head still on the pillow, and up along the leg of a table. From there, the wire ran into the back of one of the movie projectors aimed out the open glass door of the balcony.

The one bearing the threaded reels of *Motor City Pride*.

The older guy had walked March and Holly at gunpoint to the edge of the roof, where a waist-high railing was all that stood between them and a thirty-story drop. The breeze was sharp here. There was just one bird around, and it took off when it saw them coming, flapping away into the night.

Holly held on tight to her father's arm as long as she could, but when the man gestured with his gun to let him go, she did. March flopped forward onto all fours. "Ah, Christ. Help him up," the older man said, and Holly went back to his side and lifted him by one elbow again.

"Where's Tally, damn it?"

March was breathing deeply, his eyes still unfocused. "Tally who?" he mumbled. "Tally ho…" He wagged a finger in the direction of the gun.

"Why'd you have to bring the goddamn kid?" the older guy said. He seemed genuinely angry about it.

It seemed to wake March up a little. "I fucked up," he slurred.

"Yeah, you fucked up."

March started crying. Holly stood there holding onto him, biting her lip. She had to do something. It couldn't go down this way, it just couldn't.

"Go on," March slurred. "Leggo. I c'n stand."

The man waved her away with his gun and she stepped back, trying hard not to think of it as what it was, namely stepping out of the line of fire.

March swayed a bit, but stayed upright this time.

Holly looked around desperately, searching for something she could use as a weapon. But there was nothing in her reach. There was a folded wooden chair leaning against the housing of a giant ventilation fan that was maybe in her dad's reach—but a whole lot of good that was right now.

She could shout, call for help, but the bar seemed so far away, and the music was loud there, and even if she were heard, which wasn't likely, a couple of bullets could silence them both before anyone could come to their aid.

She steeled herself to do the only other thing she could think of: run at the guy, try to jump him, and almost certainly get killed in the process.

Down in the projection room, the little dial turned.

This time, a bell went *ding!* and the projector came to life, fan turning, light on, reels beginning to rotate.

In the courtyard nine stories below, a dozen loudspeakers boomed with the sound of an announcer's polished voice: "Welcome, Los Angeles, to the finest suite of automobiles Detroit has to offer!"

John-Boy went rigid, then turned his face toward the giant screen towering overhead, where an image of Bergen Paulsen standing beside an industry insignia was being replaced by footage of a 1978 Ford, first rotating in a showroom, then planted in a suburban driveway. "The word luxury redefined," the announcer recited. "In addition to the most distinctive stylings, we are bringing you interiors that are comfort assured, combining velour, leather, wood paneling, and improved…"

Up on the roof, Holly had been about to launch her run at the gunman, but the film starting below had startled her. She looked over at the gunman, hoping maybe it had startled him too, but he was a professional and didn't seem to have budged an inch. He didn't even budge when the announcer's voice abruptly cut out and the car footage ground to a stop, replaced by a counting-down film leader, the radar-sweep hand circling past 3, then 2, then cutting to a frame containing the words "THIS PICTURE IS SUITABLE ONLY FOR ADULTS."

Over the railing, Holly saw two naked bodies on the screen, a man and a woman, the man thrusting between the woman's upraised legs, and the words "A SAVAGE SID SHATTUCK PRODUCTION" emerging from the middle of the screen.

It was nothing she hadn't seen before, most recently at Shattuck's party, and it didn't faze her too much—she had more pressing things on her mind. But down below, the crowd responded with a mixture of gasps, laughter, and anger. Was this deliberate? A gag of some sort? A mistake?

The naked bodies were replaced by a medium shot of a busty brunette in a blue pinstripe outfit and black-framed glasses, sitting in a brown leather chair behind a desk that looked remarkably like Judith Kuttner's. The picture freeze-framed and went monochrome as text appeared on the screen: first *Misty Mountains in*, and then, below that, *How do you like my car, Big boy?*

Somewhere in the crowd, Bergen Paulsen exclaimed, "Oh my god."

John-Boy turned away from the screen, his steely eyes following the projection beam back to its source, the brightly lit balcony on the ninth floor. What the hell was Williams doing? This had to be dealt with before it went too far.

And up on the roof, Holland March was blubbering, wiping his eyes with his forearm.

Kingsley Williams thought it was unseemly in the extreme. He would be glad to put an end to it, frankly. Not just because it was his job to do so, not just because there was clearly no time left, but because a man like this was no man at all. Dragging his daughter into a situation she should never have been in, and then carrying on in front of her like a weakling. "You want her to see you like this? You fucking drunk." March was bawling now. "Oh, don't start that crying shit…"

March struggled to get words out between soggy gulps: "I want…"

"You drunk motherfucker, you." Williams raised his gun, aimed it squarely between the man's eyes. It was better than this asshole deserved.

March whined in Holly's direction, "I love you…"

"It's embarrassing," Williams said.

"I'm sorry baby…duck…"

"What?" Holly said.

Suddenly Holland March wasn't drunk anymore. And the wooden chair was in his hands. "Duck!" he said.

She did, and March swung the chair like Mr. October, smacking Kingsley Williams' gun out of his hand and his hand practically off his wrist. The pistol flew off into the night the way that bird had.

But it took more than a broken wrist to stop a man like Williams, and he was on March in an instant, grappling with him, forcing him bodily back, socking him with a vicious left to the midsection and a headbutt to the throat. "Motherfucker," he spat.

March tried desperately to reach his holster, and Williams tried equally desperately to pry his hand away.

If Williams hadn't been using his left against March's right, if March hadn't been only inches from his gun to start with—well, who knows. You can ask what if all night long. Point is, Williams was and March was, and the gun slid out and into March's hand, and then three bullets— one, two, three—shot out of the barrel and into the center of Williams' vest. Which got redder and redder.

Williams staggered back, arms flailing, gasping for breath. He was a dead man, just hadn't quite got there yet. Fuck. So much for raising the foundation and patching the roof, so much for the trip to Tahiti he'd been putting away for, little at a time. So much for Tally's scholarship fund. A man could hope to raise his goddaughter right, could pinch and plan, but it's the Lord decides, yes sir.

And this bastard—this March, this fucking drunk, this faker—who knew but that he'd already shot poor Tally, same way he'd just shot him?

As he fell backward, he saw Holly beside him and in an instant of vindictive fury that would cost him his entrance to Heaven, but fuck it, Saint Peter'd probably had him on a no-fly list for decades now, he grabbed Holly's arm. She was going with him, and see how Mr. Quick Draw liked that.

Without an instant's thought March launched himself at the falling man. A missile, he was a fucking missile.

He shouldered Holly out of the man's grasp, barely registered it as she dropped heavily to the roof.

Barely registered it because he realized with horror that there was nothing under him but the bullet-riddled body of a middle-aged killer in a red suit and thirty stories of air.

40.

This is what was going down on the giant movie screen as March and Williams struggled on the rooftop and then as they fell.

A porn actor in cheesy old-man makeup was leaning across Misty's desk. "Well, I'm Bulgin' Paulsen," he said, "and I represent the Detroit auto manufacturers! That's who the hell I am!"

In the crowd at the foot of the screen, the real Paulsen looked horrified. Squirmed.

On the screen, Misty rose from behind the desk, seal of the government on the wall behind her. A nameplate on the desk read *Judith Kitty-Purr*. "You poison our air! The people won't stand for it!"

"Nothin' says they can't lie down," Bulgin' Paulsen cooed.

"Well…" Misty said, "I might be persuaded to change my mind. Perhaps if we came to a *monetary* arrangement…?"

"Maybe I could put you in touch with my staff," Bulgin' Paulsen said.

"That can come later," Misty said, emphasizing the third word. This was acting at its finest. "First, I'll take wire transfers to Union Federal, account number two-two-one-two-nine. Just tell me the exact amounts to expect…I'll also need the dates and check numbers…"

"What, now?"

"Right now, big boy."

Bulgin' Paulsen looked worried. "How do I know you're not wearin' a wire?"

Misty ripped open her jacket, popping the buttons and revealing nothing underneath but her 38 triple-Ds. On the giant screen, each nipple was the height of a man. This could easily be discerned as Williams fell past one and March past the other.

"Do I look like I'm wearing a wire…?" she said.

That's what was going down.

That, and Kingsley Williams and Holland March.

41.

Splat.

42.

Ah, but that's misleading.

Williams, who had gone off the roof first, had momentum in his favor. But in colliding with him, March transferred some of that momentum to himself. He tumbled over Williams' flailing body and fell in a slightly wider arc, Williams in a slightly narrower one. It wasn't a very big difference. They only landed a few feet apart. But in Williams' case that meant hitting the tiled floor surrounding the swimming pool. In March's case it meant hitting the water.

It was all a thing of angles. Had he cannonballed in, it would probably have killed him. Landing flat would've broken his back and any number of other approaches would've snapped his neck like a twig. But what happened was, he went in clean and smooth, if not quite like Phil Boggs off the three meter at Montreal, at least like Greg Louganis off the ten.

You might wonder if March had maybe been a diver back in high school or at the police academy, but the answer is no. He hadn't even bothered to fill the pool at his rental, you'll recall. He really couldn't give a fuck about swimming or diving.

So there was no reason at all for him to survive this fall. None. Nada. It was just a matter of dumb luck. Which was really the only kind March had.

He plunged into the water, kept going, twisting and thrashing. He lost consciousness for just a second, was awakened a second later when his ass bumped hard against the bottom of the pool. Then he was blinking, blinking, trying to make sense of where he was, wondering why he was alive at all, trying to remember not to open his fucking mouth and take the deep breath he was badly craving.

Fortunately, the water was lit brightly by the searchlights outside, and he saw someone swimming toward him. A good Samaritan, surely. Someone who'd seen him fall and jumped in to help. But then the figure came closer and March could see it was a jowly, balding man in a navy business suit, and not just any jowly, balding man—it was Richard Nixon.

No. No fucking way.

March turned tail and swam as fast as he fucking could for the light at the edge of the pool.

At that instant, John-Boy was walking purposefully through the panicked crowd, toward the rotating turntable where a chesty girl in a green dress was promoting a red Chrysler. Behind him, people were shrieking—men and women alike—who'd seen Williams land or, worse, been near enough to be spattered when he did.

Well, a bit of chaos was a good thing—anyone screaming and running about wasn't watching the screen, and anyone who might have been trying to listen to the audio track would have a hard time hearing it now.

But more chaos would be even better, and with that in

mind John-Boy casually picked a mini-grenade out of his jacket pocket, pulled the pin, and slung the explosive under the Chrysler. He kept walking, briskly, unholstering an automatic weapon from under his arm as he went. When the grenade exploded a few seconds later, scattering car parts and body parts in every direction, he was already firing up at the ninth-floor window.

It took a fair number of bullets, but eventually the projector light burst and the giant projection screen went black. Finally.

Two other things happened then:

Up on the roof, Holly saw the screen go dark and ran for the elevators. This couldn't be good. She had to rescue the film. It's what her dad would've wanted.

And down in the projection room, fragments from the exploding bulb sprayed the room. One red-hot shard of glass landed on Tally's cheek, and finally she came to.

March's head broke the surface of the water just as the grenade went off, and he found himself ducking under again to avoid the shrapnel spraying through the air. When he came up for the second time, the danger had passed—or at least that danger had. There was still the danger of getting trampled by the crowds racing in every direction, plus there was the fiery wreck on the turntable, tongues of flame licking high into the air, not to mention the maniac firing an automatic pistol at the hotel building.

Wait, he knew that maniac.

With unsteady arms, March pulled himself out of the pool. There was a flattened red pile at poolside, some of it fabric, some of it human. March didn't look at it too closely. But he spotted a weapon on the edge of the pile—his own, dropped as he fell. He grabbed it, dabbled it in the pool to clean it off, and ran toward where John-Boy had just stopped shooting at the window.

He wasn't entirely sober, he realized; he hadn't been as drunk as he'd pretended when the guy had approached him with Holly at gunpoint, but he hadn't been as sober as he'd pretended when he'd gone for the home run swing with the wooden chair either. And even the fall and the dousing in the pool hadn't gotten him the rest of the way to a clear brain. But maybe that was for the best. Too much clarity wouldn't serve him well right now.

He fired off a couple of rounds in John-Boy's direction as he ran. John-Boy dropped behind a corner of the bar beside him for cover, then popped out just long enough to let loose a barrage at March. The bullets ricocheted off the side of the gold car rotating slowly on a turntable beside him. March jumped over the car's hood and slid down the other side. His heart was beating a mile a minute and his hands were shaking.

"God…God…" he heard himself saying. Fuck. Stop it, March. He sat down hard with his back to the car door, forced himself to close his eyes, take steady breaths. There was a car between him and the maniac; he was safe. All he had to do was calm down and then take his shot. Easier said than done, though—the calming down part.

"You can do this, you can do this," he told himself, squeezing his eyes tight and gripping the gun in both hands. "Three…two…one…" He spun, went up on his knees, steadied his elbows on the hood, sighted across it, and—

Where the hell was John-Boy?

For that matter, where was the bar?

A new barrage of gunfire blasted toward him from behind, glancing off the car again and very nearly cutting him in half. He tumbled sideways to get away, wound up on all fours like he had on the roof.

Fucking turntable! Though he could hardly blame the thing for, you know, turning. Fuck *him*, for not thinking of it, for letting the bastard get behind him. He rolled along the ground, came up firing, in the right direction this time, though he was hardly aiming and had no idea what he'd hit. It hadn't been John-Boy, that's for sure, since the crazy mother was striding toward him now, raising his gun—

A new barrage of gunfire erupted, but not from John-Boy's muzzle. It came from across the way, a spangled arch decorated with tinsel, where a figure stood wedged up against one side, presenting as narrow a target as possible. John-Boy dropped back, and March booked it toward the arch in a hunched-over duck walk that would've done Groucho proud.

He fell back against one leg of the arch and saw Healy pressing himself against the other, gun in hand.

"How'd you get down here?" Healy asked. "I told you to go to the roof!"

March was shaking, speechless.

"Did you *fall*?"

March thought for a moment about denying it, then decided, fuck it. "Yeah."

Healy popped out to exchange another round of gunfire with John-Boy.

"Jesus Christ," Healy said, once he was back behind the archway. "You kidding?"

"I think I'm invincible," March said. "It's the only thing that makes sense. I don't think I can die."

Healy wasn't interested in this theory. "Where's the film?" he asked.

"It's up there." March pointed up toward the now darkened ninth-floor window. "We've just got to go get it."

By the time Holly got to the projection room and burst through the door, Tally was already on her feet by the projector, sealing one of the metal film cans with electrical tape. She had a pair of scissors in one hand that she'd been using to cut the tape, and she hurled them in Holly's direction. Holly ducked just in time—she was getting good at that—and the scissors flew overhead, lodging themselves point-first in the wood of the door.

Holly ran at Tally and grabbed her around the torso, burying her face in the other woman's chest. Tally rained blows down on her back and shoulders, but Holly held on tight. Lifting one leg, Holly stomped down hard on Tally's instep, then tripped her with a kick to one calf. She let go as Tally went down. Tally wasn't the point, she reminded herself. The film was.

She snatched up the can and spun to race back to the

open door—but Tally had gotten there before her, and now had a gun pointing at her.

"Give me that," Tally said, "you fucked-up little hippie." She advanced on Holly with one arm extended for the film can.

"You want it?" Holly said. "Go get it." And like she was back at the bowling alley, she set the can down on its edge and rolled it toward the open balcony door.

Tally howled and lunged after it, but Holly stepped on the hem of her dress and she went down, slamming her head again.

And the film can—

The film can rolled onto the balcony, then off the balcony's edge, and out into space in a long, graceful arc.

43.

All eyes were on the can as it fell from the ninth-story window.

March, Healy, Paulsen, John-Boy.

It bounced once, twice, three times, before rolling to a stop on the turntable with the burning Chrysler.

Paulsen turned to the two bodyguards he'd gathered to him, both bulky men in formalwear whose neckties looked too tight, but then a loose cravat would have looked tight on necks this enormous. One of the men had a narrow mustache that he'd been trying to grow out since junior year of high school, with only limited success. His name was Afasa, and his brother's was Pati. Pati had gotten beaten up over it plenty as a kid. Not anymore. They were Samoan, and that's all Bergen Paulsen knew about them. When he called them anything, he called them "those Samoan boys." They knew he didn't know their names, but eh, bodyguarding was bodyguarding, you didn't do it for the ego strokes, you did it for the cash.

Right now, Paulsen had no need to use their names. He just pointed to where the film can had fetched up against the side of the burning wreck like a fifth hubcap. "Get me that fucking film. Move it!"

Healy saw the two enormous men break away from the crowd and go running for the can.

"Cover me," March said.

"What? What?" Healy said. "March! March—"

But March had already darted out from the cover of the archway, and was zigzagging toward the turntable. John-Boy raised his gun and got a bead on him. Healy raised his own gun, painfully conscious of how light it felt—one bullet left, probably.

He aimed as carefully as he'd ever done in his life, knowing he had to make the shot count. Pulled the trigger.

Nothing.

Well, it *had* felt light. He stuffed the gun in his pocket and started running like a tackle making for the five-yard line, yelling to get John-Boy's attention so he'd stop firing at March—his last two shots had almost hit him. But then Healy saw hotel security racing toward John-Boy as well, three of them, shouting, "Drop your weapon!" John-Boy swerved to face them, and Healy tacked left to go after the bodyguards instead.

Behind him, the three security guards leaped on John-Boy before he could fire at them, but it was a doomed attempt. Three against one would seem to be good odds, but John-Boy made swift work of them, grabbing one around the neck and ramming him headfirst into the second. The third he grabbed in an armlock and then snapped the man's elbow over his knee.

Healy didn't see this happen. He'd climbed up onto a table and used it for a launching platform for a flying leap onto the backs of Pati and Afasa. The three went down in a heap. Healy began laying about himself with punches to both men's faces, hoping for a knockout before it could turn into a proper fight.

March didn't see either of these skirmishes. All he saw was the metal film can, and he grabbed it before working through the equation that metal plus fire equals hot. He dropped it again, blew on his burned fingers.

Then he looked up, only to see Healy kneeling on the chest of one of the bodyguards, dealing out punches. "March! Go!" he shouted. "I've got this!" March turned back to the can, took another grab at it, wedging it under his arm this time so it wouldn't singe his skin.

He felt his armpit warm up. It felt sort of nice, actually.

He didn't see the second bodyguard rear up behind Healy and take him down with a punch to the neck.

He did see John-Boy rearing up from the pile of downed security guards, though. The tall man brushed off his pant legs, checked his gun, then casually put a bullet in each guard's head.

That was enough to send March running, scurrying back into the nearer of the hotel towers. There were escalators to take you to the Grand Ballroom upstairs or the parking level underground. Neither sounded great, but he shot up the former, taking the steps two at a time. He heard slapping shoe-leather beneath him, and glancing down saw John-Boy aiming back up. A bullet ricocheted against the wall by March's head and he was off, running again. Another escalator up—then one down—

How long could he keep this up? John-Boy was younger and faster, and crazier. And armed. March had dropped his own gun somewhere along the way, probably when he'd picked up the film can. Not that he could've done a good job of carrying both anyway, but he still wished he had it on him. Guns made everything better. When they were yours. Not so much when they were, you know, a hired killer's.

March jumped over the side of the escalator he was currently on, landing on a banquet table, which upended under him, dumping him on the ground. From behind it came gunshots, and bullet holes appeared in the wood of the table over his head. He got to his feet again and sprinted, the film can clutched to his chest.

But now he was out in the open, and he was running out of places to, well, run. This was the level that exited onto the glass walkway connecting the two towers, and March made for that. But where was the fucking door? He reached a huge plate glass window overlooking the walkway, hammered on it with one fist in frustration— then saw it shatter to a million pieces.

Did I do that? He spun, saw John-Boy standing behind him, his gun extended and smoking. Nope. *He* did that.

March caught the next bullet in his chest—or would have, if the film can hadn't been in the way. The bullet lodged in the center of the film, but the impact threw March backward, through the blasted window and out onto the walkway.

He lost hold of the can as he fell, and saw it roll, on end, toward the edge. He crawled after it, one arm outstretched, desperately trying to get it before it—

The can bounced over the edge and down to a lower level, landing on a glass floor through which March could see the tops of cars passing below on the parking level. He hurled himself over the edge after it.

The can had bounced and rolled on the glass, but that

was because the can weighed, what, two pounds? Four? Ten? March went one-fifty-five on a good day, and when he hit the glass he smashed right through, landing with a shower of fragments on the roof of the car beneath him. The metal buckled, and all the air was driven out of March's body. He groaned and just lay face down for a second, trying to breathe. But the can had fallen through with him, hit the pavement, and it was still rolling.

March forced himself to get up, slide off the roof. He staggered out into the road, chasing after the can, dodging a honking taxicab and caroming off the grill of a town car. Thank god they were all driving slowly down here.

He had the can in sight—still rolling, but not far away—when he was shoulder-checked from behind by a fucking linebacker in a necktie who knocked him to the ground and went chasing after the can himself.

March staggered to his feet again, then ducked back when a gunshot from the walkway passed close enough to part his hair. Risking a glance back, he saw John-Boy up there, taking aim for another.

Then someone behind John-Boy shouted "Hey!" and the gunman spun.

Healy landed on his shoulder, took him down to the surface of the walkway.

March allowed himself a smile. Just a small one. Then ran after the fucking can.

On the walkway, Healy and John-Boy were rolling around in broken glass, trading punches. It was brutal, but in some strange way nostalgic, too. There were backlots in the Bronx where the best thing you could hope to land on during a fight was a rusty nail, where broken glass was not in short supply and more than once had been used deliberately to inflict damage. Healy had seen throats cut. The kids he grew up with hadn't been playing. You learned to fight young or you moved the hell out of the Bronx.

Healy hadn't moved.

Which didn't mean he enjoyed getting punched in the face, in the jaw, in the chest. But it meant he could take it, and he could dish it out, and even when this psycho got him in a choke hold, Healy on his knees, John-Boy standing behind him with a powerful forearm around his neck, he knew a trick or two he hadn't taught to his students at the Learning Adjunct. Reaching back with both arms, he jammed his hands into John-Boy's jacket pockets, gripped tight, and flipped the bastard forward over his head. The guy landed face down inches from the edge of the walkway, and Healy expected him to be out of commission for at least a beat or two, long enough for Healy to take him out with a kick to the head. But no—the guy jumped up again instantly. Fuck.

Healy clenched his hands into fists again. He felt something in his hand, on his finger, something that had come out of John-Boy's pocket when he flipped him, and looking down, Healy saw what it was.

He held it up for John-Boy to see, too.

And for the first time he saw fear in the man's eyes.

March was running, trying to get to Afasa, who was inches from the rolling can. One car cut in front of March, who dodged and suddenly found himself flat on his back on the hood of another. Behind him, he heard the woman in the driver's seat shriek. She hit the gas by accident, driving March forward a few yards, then stomped the brake. March sailed off the front of the car, hit the ground running—well, on his feet, anyway, momentum carrying him forward, and he rammed into Afasa from behind, tackling him around the knees. Both men went down. Afasa had grabbed the can, but now it slipped from his fingers and, damn it, went rolling again. March smacked Afasa's forehead into the pavement, then climbed over him to get to the can—but a gunshot from behind struck the pavement beside him. John-Boy…? March risked a look back, and saw Afasa's brother standing near one of the hotel exits, in the shadow of the walkway overhead, gun extended in one hand. He looked furious at what March had done to his brother.

March raised both arms before him. Could his cast block a bullet like the film can had? Somehow he doubted it. But what else did he have? He couldn't run anymore. He was done.

Something going on over Pati's head caught March's eye then. It was John-Boy, and he looked like he was desperately trying to get out of his jacket. He whipped one arm out of one sleeve, then found himself tangled in the other. He angrily yanked it off, tearing the fabric in the process, and hurled the whole thing over the edge.

It landed on Pati's outstretched arm.

Pati looked up, startled and annoyed. But only for a second.

March dropped, pressed his face into the pavement, covered his head with both arms.

✥

The thing dangling from Healy's finger was a grenade pin.

He turned and ran, dropping behind a planter and waiting for the explosion.

He wasn't disappointed.

At least until he peeked around the corner and saw John-Boy still standing, in his shirtsleeves, watching the aftermath of the explosion down below.

At least the son of a bitch was distracted. Healy would take what he could get. He ran from behind the planter and got John-Boy around the waist. Wheeled him around, gave him a knee to the gut, another to the groin, took him down to the ground. Straddled him. Gave him the old one-two, right across the chops, only it was the old one-two-three-four-five-six-seven-eight by the time Healy had finished. Then he shot out his right hand, cinched it around the man's throat, and started squeezing.

It was good enough for Dufresne, motherfucker. It's good enough for you.

John-Boy struggled. This was a tough guy, all right. But Healy was a tough guy too, and this time he had the leverage. He leaned forward, put his weight into it.

"Mr. Healy! What are you doing!"

Looking up, Healy saw a wisp of a girl standing in the doorway, her eyes wide. Horrified.

"Go away, Holly."

John-Boy was writhing under him. His face was turning purple.

"Healy, stop! You don't have to kill him!"

Oh, but I do, Holly. You don't understand. A guy like

this? He can't be cured. He's rotten to the core. Evil. You can't fix him. You can't improve him.

"Mr. Healy," Holly said, "if you kill this man, I will never speak to you again."

He looked at her. Looked down at his hand, locked around John-Boy's throat.

He deserves it.

It was true: he did. And the world deserved to be rid of him. And he couldn't be cured, couldn't be fixed, couldn't be improved. It was all true, every last word of it.

But something spoke to Healy, in that moment, a little voice in his head. He thought later that maybe it was Scotty, his sponsor, but that was only because he refused—refused—to believe it was his dad's voice. And what this voice said was, *You're right. You're right. Simple as that— you're right. He can't be improved. But you know who can? You can.*

You fucking can.

He let up on the pressure, and under him John-Boy started choking, gasping for air.

"Congratulations, buddy," Healy muttered. "You owe your life to a thirteen-year-old girl."

John-Boy's eyes were closed. He was still struggling to breathe. It's okay. It wasn't important that he hear it. It was only important that Healy could say it.

Healy raised his fist, took aim, and slammed it into the bastard's temple. His head smacked the concrete and he was down at last. Still breathing raggedly, but shallower now that he was unconscious.

"Good night, John-Boy," Healy said.

◦

March was on his feet again. How, he didn't know. But the can was still rolling and so was he. His jacket was singed from the explosion, his hair too. But Pati had gotten it worse, obviously. So March wasn't complaining.

He saw the can finally tip on its side and fall clattering to the pavement, and he staggered over to it, ignoring the sound of another explosion behind him. Who the fuck knew what that one was. Maybe someone was still shooting at him. Maybe Detroit had just rolled out a new car of the future and one of the features was, it exploded. You know, on command. Fuck it. There was the film. There were his fingers. He lifted the can, hugged it to his chest. End of the line.

Looking down at his hand, he saw the words that had been scrawled onto his skin were still there, just fainter and smudged. One word in particular was smudged to the point of being unreadable, and seeing that made him grin. The missing word was *never*. The sentence now said *You will…be happy.* Well, fuck me. If that isn't a sign, I don't know what is.

"Dad!"

He looked up, saw Healy and Holly looking down from the edge of the walkway.

Holly was in tears.

No, baby, he wanted to say, don't cry, I made it. We made it. See?

He held the film can up over his head. Smiled at her. Crooked his pinky in her direction.

He limped toward the building, but gave up halfway

there. There was a car with smashed windows stopped slantwise across the road. It wasn't going anywhere. March sank down beside it, laid his head back against the driver's door, set the film can down against his thigh.

In the distance, he heard sirens.

"And that," he said softly to himself, "would be the cops."

He reached into his jacket pocket, came back out with his lighter and a cigarette.

He was smoking it with a look of deep satisfaction on his face when the cop cars drove in.

Sometimes, you just win.

44.

But not this time.

45.

In the lobby of the courthouse, March and Healy were seated side by side. They both looked up when the doors swung open, thinking maybe it was Perry, come to tell them they could go. It wasn't.

"Jesus Christ," March said.

"Oh, shit," was Healy's version of the sentiment.

"You know what?" March said. "Don't even talk to her. Don't even look at her, man."

A uniformed guard led Judith Kuttner down the hallway toward where they were sitting, then gestured for her to sit, too. At least the guard sat her facing the other way, their backs to each other. They wouldn't have to look her in the face, or she them. They certainly didn't have to talk.

But then she spoke to them.

Without looking their way, it was true. But there was no one else there. She wasn't talking to the guard. Especially given that she started by saying, "Oh, boys, boys…you really think you got something done here."

Healy and March looked at each other. Didn't look at her.

Kuttner's voice dripped with condescension. "Do you have a clue what just happened? This wasn't some plan I had on my own. It was protocol. I followed protocol."

March started grunting something in German, or what had passed for German on Sid Caesar.

"What's wrong with him?" she said, turning to look at them.

"I believe," Healy said, "he's making a connection between you and Adolf Hitler." He smiled in her direction.

She turned away again. Spoke to the wall across from her. "Read the fucking newspaper," she said, slowly and with bitterness, like the world's angriest history teacher. "What's good for Detroit is good for America. The America I love owes its life to the big three."

"And who did your daughter owe her life to?" Healy said.

"Detroit had her killed!" Kuttner said.

March nodded. "I think you're right about that. The whole city got together, took a vote. Big turnout."

"I wanted her safe!" Kuttner spat. "That's why I hired you two."

Well, that hit home just a bit. Maybe it shouldn't have, but it did.

Healy cleared his throat. "Uh, you're going to jail, Mrs. Kuttner. Not us."

"I might be going to jail," she said, "but it won't make a difference. You can't take Detroit down. If I'm not there to take care of it, someone else will be."

"Okay," March said, letting that sink in. "Well. We shall see."

46.

March had a new Mercedes convertible, chocolate-brown with a smooth purring engine, so there was that, at least. You took your victories where you could find them.

He drove past the Comedy Store, pulled in at a nearby cocktail lounge, past a bell-ringing Santa Claus and a loudspeaker pouring Kay Starr into the sunshine of an L.A. December: *Old Mr. Kringle is soon gonna jingle the bells that'll tingle all your troubles away…*

Yes, Halloween had come and gone in the middle of all that nonsense, Thanksgiving had flown by, and now here it was Christmas again, the season of joy, and if anyone was looking joyful it wasn't the people sitting at this bar in the middle of the afternoon. March walked in, his attention on the cute bartender in the off-the-shoulder peasant blouse, then did a double take when he saw his daughter sitting on a stool near the door, waiting for him. "Jesus," he said.

"It's just Coke," Holly said, raising the glass in her hand. Yeah, just Coke if you didn't count the rum-and. But fuck it. She was a teenager now, and more than that, she was the most responsible person he knew. Plus, it was Christmas.

"Where is he?" March asked, and Holly pointed to a stool at the bar. A man sat bent over a fifth of something amber colored. March walked over, hung over his shoulder until Healy noticed him. It took a while.

March couldn't believe his eyes. Healy was drunk. Probably stinking drunk, but at least March didn't have to endure that. Not to mention the smell of the half-smoked cigar clenched between Healy's teeth.

March sat down on the next stool over, raised an index finger. "Scotch," he said, and gave the bartender a smile.

Healy, slurring his words something awful, said, "You see the TV?"

"Yeah," March said. "I saw it."

The girl behind the bar brought him his drink.

"They're gonna let them off, the car companies. Scot-free," Healy said.

March lit a cigarette, took a long drag.

Healy continued his lament. " 'Not enough evidence of collusion.' They say."

"I heard."

"Sun went up, sun went down. Nothing changes. Just like you said." Healy punctuated his words with jabs of the cigar.

"Look," March said. "They got away with it. Big surprise. You know? People are stupid." He swallowed some more of his whiskey. "But they're not that stupid. The point is, five years, tops, we're all driving electric cars from Japan anyway. Mark my words."

Healy didn't seem mollified. Jesus. This was as bad as March had ever seen him, and that included the day he'd broken March's arm.

"Look at this," he said, "you ever see the bad breath tie?" He lifted his necktie so the tip was pointing straight up in his hand. He exhaled on the end. Nothing. Stuck it in front of Healy's mouth. "Breathe on it." Healy exhaled. The end of the tie wilted as March moved his thumb.

Healy started laughing. God, that was stupid. But a classic's a classic.

"Works every time," March said. "Kills Holly."

Healy's laughter had petered out, but he gave March a little smile.

"At least you're drinking again," March said.

"Yeah. Feel great."

"What is that, Dewar's?"

"It ain't Yoo-hoo."

March tossed back the rest of his drink, signaled for another. "You know, we did okay. Nobody got hurt—"

"Well," Healy muttered. "A few people got hurt."

"I'm saying I think they died quickly, though, so I don't think that they got *hurt*." March took something from his pocket. It was an ad torn from the Yellow Pages. He laid it on the bar in front of Healy. "Look at this," he said. Healy bent close to look.

The ad hadn't changed much. It still said "Our trained investigators have specialized in CLOSING CASES since 1972" and "24-Hour Service" and "Licensed and Bonded." But up at the top it now said THE NICE GUYS AGENCY, and instead of just one little drawing, of March's face, there were two little drawings, one of each of them. Healy squinted.

"I'm sorry you look Filipino," March said.

"I do. Or…Mexican."

"And hey," March said, "we already got our first case. Old lady in Glendale."

"Mm-hm," said Healy.

"Thinks her husband is sleeping with Lynda Carter."

"Wonder Woman?"

"...or Lynda Carter. That's what we have to figure out."

"Right," said Healy.

"But he's eighty-two, so it's time sensitive."

"Mm-hm."

"What do you say?"

Before Healy could say anything, March jumped up, snatched the ad off the bar and started slapping it down in front of him. "Shit! Shit!" Then he pressed the ad down hard, his thumb grinding something underneath it.

"What...?"

March cleared his throat. "Bee."

"Uh-huh."

The bartender came, and March gave her a wink as he took the scotch glass from her. Was there potential there? There was potential everywhere.

He raised the glass in Healy's direction. "To the birds?" he said.

Healy raised his bottle. They clinked.

"Hallelujah," he said, and drank to his new career.